The Summer of El Pintor

Ofelia Dumas Lachtman

Arte Público Press
Houston, Texas

This volume is made possible through grants from the National Endowment for the Arts (a federal agency), Andrew W. Mellon Foundation, and the City of Houston through The Cultural Arts Council of Houston, Harris County.

Recovering the past, creating the future

Arte Público Press
University of Houston
452 Cullen Performance Hall
Houston, Texas 77204-2004

Cover design by Ken Bullock
Cover illustration and line art by Pauline Rodriguez Howard

Lachtman, Ofelia Dumas.
    The Summer of El Pintor / by Ofelia Dumas Lachtman.
        p.   cm.
    Summary: When sixteen-year-old Monica and her widowed father go back to Los Angeles, reluctantly moving from a wealthy neighborhood to the barrio house her mother grew up in, Monica tries to locate a missing neighbor, and in the process learns about her mother's past.
    ISBN 1-55885-327-8 (pbk.)
    [1. Identify—Fiction. 2. Moving, Household—Fiction. 3. Single-parent familes—Fiction. 4. Mexican Americans—Fiction. 5. Los Angeles (Calif.)—Fiction. 6. Mystery and detective stories.]   I. Title
PZ7.L13535 Su 2001
[Fic]—dc21   00-069281
                                                                    CIP

5 6 7 8 9 0 1 2 3 4   10 9 8 7 6 5 4 3 2

For Alan, Alissa, and Bryan.

Thanks for the cool answers.

Chapter One

Monica Ramos was glad that her father couldn't read her thoughts. She leaned forward in the passenger seat of the gray BMW and glanced at him. Apparently intent on the traffic ahead on Dennison Boulevard, he sat hunched over the steering wheel. The sun struggled to push through the overcast skies of a June morning in Los Angeles. Monica cleared her throat—she didn't want her voice to give any of her glum thoughts away—and said, "We're not there yet, are we?"

"Close," he said. "Another mile or so." Her father was a tall man in his late forties, olive-skinned, dark-eyed, handsome. His face was long and thin; he didn't look at all like her. Her face was oval; her eyes light brown, almost hazel; and her shoulder-length hair was light brown, too. She turned away, staring uneasily at the small shabby buildings that lined the street.

When they passed Grace's Café, the aroma of burgers and french fries reached her, reminding her that it was almost lunch time and that she was hungry. But not for food from Grace's, she thought with a little shake of her head. Even the windows look greasy. Next to Grace's was The Bright Hope Thrift Shop, showing in its display window a turquoise wool

1

suit on a headless mannequin and a row of well-polished women's shoes. When they stopped at a street called Bell Avenue, she saw that one corner of the intersection was taken up by a furniture store that displayed a banner shouting, *¡Venta!* Sale! in bold red letters. The other three corners were filled by a beauty shop called *La Princesa, García*'s Drug and Sundries, and Mónica's Boutique. Monica. With an accent. If my name ever had an accent, she thought, it doesn't now and I like it that way.

Her father was looking around, too. He shook his head and said, "My god, it's been at least ten years, and nothing's changed."

Monica stared at him. "You mean you knew the neighborhood was going to be like this?" What she thought and didn't say was, this is a barrio.

"More or less."

"And you still chose to come here?" She had visions of gangs and guns and nights of terror.

"Choice had nothing to do with it, Monica. Luck did. We're lucky the tenants cleared out because this little house of your mother's is all we own in the world now."

"You mean we're going to be here all summer?"

"It looks that way."

"And longer?"

"Yes, Monica, probably longer."

"What'll I do about school then?"

Her father sighed. "The worst that can happen is that you'll go to the same high school your mother went to, Talbot High. Things have changed, Monica. You've got to begin to understand that."

"I'm trying to," Monica said and turned to look out of the window. Yes, I'm trying, she thought, but it's hard to understand when your world has been yanked out from under you. She had expected to have a shiny new car of her own this summer, and not getting it was just the beginning of her disappointments. She sat silently, thinking once again of all that had happened in the last year.

It had started that awful morning at her boarding school in Fairmount, Virginia. She had been dozing, half-listening to the morning sounds of Raeburn School when her roommate Courtney pulled open their bedroom door, tossed a newspaper onto her bed, and said, "Your dad has resigned. If he wasn't guilty, why would he do that?"

She had wondered the same thing even after her father had explained two or three times that an investigation would embarrass his superiors—and probably would do no good.

"But you're innocent," she argued.

"Yes," he said, "too innocent. That was the trouble. I was too naïve, too eager, easy prey for the buzzards that hover over our capital city. Things might have been different if your mother was alive; she might have seen what I didn't. I know I didn't mishandle those funds. Politics," he added with a shrug, "is a tough game."

"I don't care," Monica insisted. "It isn't fair."

"Monica," he had said finally in that reasoning tone that drove her crazy, "everything isn't always fair. All I can tell you now is that it took every penny I had to pay my legal fees. Somebody was bound to go."

So her father, Eduardo Ramos, had resigned from his highly placed government job and returned to California, leaving her to finish her already-paid-for year at school.

From that day on, Raeburn wasn't the same. No more limos came to take her to special events with her dad. No more resourceful reporters sought her. There was no more envy in the glances of her schoolmates. Some of their glances held disdain; others, pity. Day by miserable day, the last two months of the semester dragged by. Finally, June came, and she flew to Los Angeles to start a new life with her father. All in all, she had looked forward to that. Of course, Washington and a fancy boarding school like Raeburn were exciting, but she hadn't seen her dad enough, and she missed the closeness they had always had. Still, she hadn't expected her new life to start in this kind of a neighborhood. Before her dad's appointment, they had lived in a two-story house in Los Angeles on a street called Parkview Place that had lovely gardens and tall trees. They hadn't been rich, she knew that, but her father's law practice had provided everything they needed, including Rosa, who had come to care for her and the house after her mother's death.

She was jolted out of her thoughts when the car made a sudden sharp turn onto a side street. "This is Lucia Street," her dad said. "Almost missed it. There used to be a guitar shop on the corner."

"There still is," Monica said, glancing over her shoulder. "A tiny one-story place."

"With a huge black-and-gold guitar on the roof?"

"No. Nothing. Just a sign over the windows that says, Salcedo and Sons."

"So they're still there," he said with a smile. "Wonder what happened to the guitar?"

"Maybe an earthquake," Monica said. Or maybe, she thought, they got good sense and took it down.

"Maybe," her father answered, and they were silent.

Lucia was a narrow street lined with small houses fronted by dry patches of lawn. Old pepper trees, whose branches hung limply over the scattered red berries below them, grew alongside the curbs. On a dusty driveway two teenage boys in grease-spotted T-shirts were working on a torn-down car. They shot glances in their direction.

Monica shrank into the black leather of the bucket seat. She wanted to hide. But why? She took a deep breath, sat up, and forced herself to look around again.

The morning mist was completely gone. The sun was strong and bright, intensifying the color of a row of potted marigolds on the front porch of one of the houses. A dog squeezed through a broken picket fence out onto the street, interrupting the ball game of four small boys. When the boys caught sight of the car, they scrambled toward the curb, where they stared at them with obvious curiosity. Monica waved and the smallest of the four, a thin, brown-skinned boy with a red baseball cap pulled backwards behind large ears, grinned and waved back.

Her dad made an abrupt U-turn and pulled over to the curb. "Here we are," he said.

The house they stopped at was gray—or was it a dirty tan?—with four or five steps that led to a narrow front porch. On the wall beyond the porch a faded green shutter hung crookedly beside a large window. The house was small and much like the other houses on the block except in one respect: Where all the other houses had driveways that extended from the street along the side of the house and into the garage, this driveway was filled halfway by a long, narrow addition to the garage. The front of this addition looked like a child's drawing of a house. There was a grape-colored door in the center, two windows on either side of the door, and below each window, a neatly painted turquoise-colored bench. Stepping stones led from the purple door to the sidewalk through a garden of low-growing flowers.

Monica looked from the colorful little plot to the dingy house next to it, then turned and said, "Yes, here we are, but where? Which of the two is ours?"

"Two? Oh, you mean the studio. No, that's not for us. That's where Mr. Mead, El Pintor, lives."

"You mean somebody rents that little building?"

"No. I mean somebody lives there without paying rent. And he can for as long as he wants. That's the agreement your mother's family made with him. Your mother respected that. And we will, too."

"Okay, okay, Dad. You don't have to be so preachy. I didn't say you should evict him."

Her father grinned. "Was I sermonizing? Sorry about that. Come on, let's go see what the house is like."

When she got out of the car, Monica paused and said, "El Pintor, h-m-m. The painter. Why didn't he paint our house, too?"

"He's not that kind of a painter," her father said. "He's an artist. He paints on canvas."

Monica shrugged, and they went up the short walkway and the porch steps. "Those chairs," she said, pointing to a pair of woven plastic chairs on the porch. "They're just like the ones we had by the fish pond on Parkview."

"They are, aren't they?" he said and unlocked the door. He held the door for her, and she went inside.

There was no entry hall. She had stepped directly into the living room. As she looked around the room, tears pushed into her eyes. "Oh, Dad," she said with a smile, "you took our things out of storage."

"Not everything," he said. "This house is too small."

She nodded. This room was furnished with the rattan furniture from their old den. And the adjoining dining room had the breakfast room table and chairs. She was secretly glad; she never had liked the ornate dining room chairs that everyone claimed were so priceless. When she found her bedroom, she stopped at the door and drew in her breath. The room was filled with all her things, up to and including the mound of cushions on her bed and the curtains on the windows.

"This is great!" she cried. "Dad, how did you ever find the time?"

"I didn't," her father said. He put the suitcases he was carrying by the bedroom door. "I did arrange with Tim Lacy, our old handyman, to paint the inside of the house, but as for all this, the answer is Rosa. When the business I had in Florida held me up, I called Rosa and asked if she could be here when they delivered our things last Saturday." He paused and shook his head. "And this is the result."

"She must've spent the whole weekend here."

"I'm sure."

"Do you suppose the refrigerator's running? And do you suppose there's some food in it? I'm starving."

"Let's find out."

The refrigerator was running, and there was food. "There's enough stuff here for a month," Monica said. "Even some of Rosa's great vegetable soup." Her dad was shaking his head again, and she added, "Can we pay her for all this?"

He gave her a quick hug and said, "I've had a few good commissions here and there across the country. Don't you worry about that. Come on, let's eat before we start unpacking."

It took a couple of hours for Monica to empty her two suitcases and distribute their contents in the chest of drawers and the tiny closet. When she was done, she held open the closet door and looked with dismay at the almost-filled rod that held her clothes. Where would she put the rest of her clothes when they arrived? For that matter, where would she put her TV? Her boom box? She closed the closet door abruptly and sat on the floor, her back against the side of the bed. Everything's changed so much, she thought. I knew it would be different. But not this different. She sat another few minutes staring at the opposite wall, then got up and wandered through the rest of the house.

Beyond the kitchen there was a screen porch where a washing machine and dryer waited to be installed. Her father was at the hardware store hoping to find the right fittings to complete the job. She went into the kitchen and sat down at a small, plastic-topped table that was pushed against the wall. Here in this very room, maybe in this very corner, her mother had spent many hours. Monica stared at the kitchen window and at the sunlight that angled through it to the sink. How many times had her mother stood there, looking out that window? Being in this house, Monica had thought she would have a sense of her, a feeling of what she was like, but there was nothing yet. She knew so little about her. Four years old was not old enough to remember much, and that's what she'd been when her mother died. But she did have one memory, and that memory was as sweet as birthday cake. She closed her eyes, and the incident played through her mind in clear, bright images. A radiant summer day. A gentle ocean breeze. Wind chimes tinkling by the patio door. Her mother in a flowered skirt and a pretty white top hurrying across the grass of the backyard with a gray kitten held tenderly in her hands. "*Mira, mira, mi'jita, mira lo que tengo aquí.*" Look, look, little daughter, look what I have here. Six months later her mother was dead, but the gray cat Willy had lived for many years.

Monica sighed. The sun had moved from the window, and the room felt cold and forlorn. She rose and went through the house to the front porch. There she walked to the edge of the steps and, leaning against the porch pillar, glanced up and down the street. Everything she saw seemed dingy. Even the sunshine had a dusty edge. The ball game was over and the players were now on the sidewalk racing on noisy skateboards. A pair of scruffy little dogs ran back and forth after them, barking loudly. The teenage boys with the torn-down car were no longer alone. Two girls in skin-tight jeans and halter tops leaned against the car. As Monica watched, the girls squealed and ran to the center of the street, and the boy who had been threatening them with greasy hands, followed them to the curb and laughed.

"Come on back," he called. "This ain't bad grease. No worse than that stuff on your faces."

The girls shrugged and giggled and said something that Monica couldn't hear because someone close by called, "Hey, you! I'm talking to you!" Standing by the steps below her was the little ball player with the red cap.

"I'm sorry," Monica said. "I didn't hear you. What did you say?"

"Did you bring El Pintor?"

"Did we what?"

"El Pintor. Did you bring him?"

"El Pintor? You mean the man who lives over there?" She indicated the little house on the driveway. When the boy nodded, she shook her head and added, "No, we didn't bring him. Why should we?"

"Well, when is he gonna come back then?"

"I don't know. I don't know anything about him."

"Man!" the boy said with a disgusted frown. He yanked the cap off his head and threw it on the ground. "Man," he repeated, "nobody knows nothing!"

"Sorry," Monica said. "I've got to go in now." She paused by the screen door and watched the boy cross the street. When he reached the opposite curb, he turned, looked at her, and gave a sad little shrug. Funny kid, she thought as she pulled open the screen door. I hope he's not going to be a pest. Inside, she walked straight through the house to the back door and out into the backyard.

At the bottom of the wooden steps she stopped and looked around. If there had been grass in the rectangular yard at one time, it had long despaired of growing; only a brownish stubble covered the ground. A white wooden fence, its paint peeling, ran along the right side of the yard. On the ground along the fence, leggy geraniums struggled to bloom, and in a rear corner of the yard, a glossy-leafed lemon tree dotted with fruit glistened in the sunlight. Straggling geraniums grew also at the side of the garage. Monica walked to them, bent over, and picked two of the blood-red blooms. She was surprised to discover that the garage was not connected to the "studio," as her dad had called it.

Rather, there was a six-foot space between the two buildings, allowing the garage doors room in which to swing open. The studio was about a story-and-a-half-high, with a row of small windows near the roof line along its side and across the back. Below the windows on the back wall, a door stood open.

A girl clad in white shorts and a sleeveless blue shirt backed out of the door. She was making a murmuring sound like a lullaby as she moved, bent over, through the opening. Monica started to say something, but instead took a step back, as if to give the newcomer more room. At her movement, the girl in the door straightened up and whirled around.

Monica stared at her. She had an interesting face, sharply chiseled under a cap of curly black hair. She looks about my age, Monica thought.

For an instant the girl stared back, her jaw slack. Then her eyes widened, and her face grew pale beneath her coppery tan. "You! Why, you're . . . you're 'Springtime!'" she said breathlessly.

Chapter Two

Three questions struck Monica at once: Spring-time? What're you talking about? And who are you? She asked none of them. What she said was, "Is something wrong?"

The girl didn't answer immediately. First she looked back to the shadowy interior of the studio, then over Monica's shoulder to the lemon tree, then back to meet Monica's eyes. "I . . . but you . . . I guess you're not . . . but I . . ." Her face reddened as she stammered. Finally, she blurted out, "What're you doing here, anyway?"

"I live here," Monica said crisply. "Do you? In the studio, I mean?"

"No." The girl edged toward the open door. "But I'm a friend of the man who does. And right now I'm trying to get Sopa to come outside."

"Sopa?"

"Sopa's the cat that lives here. But she's going to starve to death if I don't get her out of there."

"Why? Doesn't he feed her?"

"He would if he was here." The girl bent over in the doorway once more and began her wheedling little lullaby. "Sopita, Sopita, Sopita, *ven, ven, ven acá.*"

Monica walked to a spot behind her and looked over her shoulder. Inside the studio, not two yards away, sat the cat. She was a calico patchwork cat, orange, brown, and black. Her yellow eyes stood out like headlights as she stared, unmoving, at the girl.

"Why don't you just go pick her up?" Monica whispered.

"Not Sopa. I'd get clawed to death."

Monica shrugged. "What makes you think she's starving?"

"Because." The girl straightened up and sighed. "Because she's been locked in there for almost a week."

"Maybe she ate mice. My cat Willy used to catch them."

"Not Sopa. She'd starve to death first. She won't even eat canned pet food. What she really goes for is people food, especially soup. And not canned soup either."

Monica grinned. "Is that why she's called Sopa?" The girl grinned, too, and nodded. "How does she like her soup?" Monica asked. "Kind of warm? Like the leftovers in a plate?"

"I don't know. Why?"

"Because I happen to have soup. Homemade. And even if she wasn't starving, she'd love Rosa's soup."

"Who's Rosa? Your mother?"

"Uh-uh. Our housekeeper."

"Your *what?*"

"I mean she was our housekeeper," Monica said and felt the blood rising to her face. "Do you want the soup or don't you?"

"Okay. Sure. We can give it a try."

Monica went quickly up the steps. In just a few minutes she returned with a cup of vegetable soup in one hand, a saucer in the other. "Willy always liked slurpy stuff out of a saucer," she said and knelt by the studio door. She poured some soup into the saucer, edged it onto the threshold, and got up. The cat, she was sure, had not moved a muscle, had not even blinked, while she did that. She took a couple of steps back and said, "Maybe if we leave her alone, she'll eat." She turned to the girl. "My name's Monica. What's yours?"

"Toni. Really Antonia. Antonia Almayo. How come you know so much about cats?"

"Not 'cats.' Cat. Just Willy. He was kind of fat and friendly, but he sure hated to have people close when he ate."

They turned and leaned against the garage doors and stared at the cat, who had yet to move. Monica's eyes were on Sopa, but she was seeing Willy. She was seeing the fish pond, too—the fish pond without fish because of Willy. And beyond the pond she saw the reds and pinks of the azaleas that bordered the back lawn on Parkview Place. A lump pushed into her throat, leaving an empty, hollow place in her chest that she knew was homesickness. She recognized it because it had happened, too, when they went to Washington, D.C. Of course, there the excitement had quickly filled the empty place. But here there was nothing to—here there was just plain nothing. She gave a quick little shake of her head. Enough of that. She was here, and, little as she liked it, she'd have to get used to it.

"Look, look!" Toni whispered. "She's going to eat."

The patchwork cat was at the wooden threshold. She bent over the saucer, peered at them with appraising golden eyes, then took a tentative slurp. She shot another look at them, and then returned to the soup.

"I gave her just a little bit," Monica whispered. "When she's done, we'll drag the saucer out a foot or two and fill it again."

By the time the cup of soup was gone, Toni had pulled the studio door closed, Monica had moved to sit on the lowest of her back steps, and Sopa was eating from the saucer close to her feet.

Toni, who stood a couple of yards away, watched the cat with disbelief. After a while she said, "Do you think you could take care of Sopa for a while? She's obviously taken a liking to you."

"Not me. It's the soup."

"It's both," Toni said firmly. "She hardly ever makes friends."

Monica reached down and scratched the cat behind the ears. "So how long would I have to take care of her?"

"Until El Pintor comes back."

"When'll that be?"

A troubled frown clouded Toni's face. "I don't know. That's the trouble."

"It doesn't matter," Monica said. "I'll watch her. She'll hang around here, anyway. Cats are pretty territorial."

"That's really nice," Toni said. "Thanks. Now I've got to get back."

"No, you don't!" Monica said and shot up, sending Sopa streaking to the center of the yard, where she turned and looked speculatively at both of them. "Not until you explain that 'Springtime' thing. Unless you want me to think you're crazy."

"Maybe I am," Toni said slowly. Then she cocked her head, took a long look at her, and said, "Come on. Come see what you think." Pulling a key out of her pocket, she headed for the studio door. She threw the door open.

Monica hesitated. "Is it all right for us to go in?" she asked. Long ago, when she and a friend had walked into a neighbor's garage uninvited, her father had given her a stern lecture on trespassing. She had never forgotten it.

"Sure, it's all right," Toni said. "This is my key. I've been cleaning his place since I was ten. At first I did it for nothing, or mostly nothing. Just for the paper and paints and little books he gave me. But pretty soon he said that people shouldn't sell themselves short. That they should receive pay worthy of their efforts—or something like that. Anyway, he's paid me ever since." She tapped Monica on the arm. "Go on. Go ahead."

Monica stepped inside. She was standing in a high-ceilinged room with a long, narrow table pushed against one wall. On the table were sketch pads neatly stacked, a ceramic bowl filled with paint brushes, upended, and another that held an assortment of art pencils. On the floor, three easels faced the doorway. They held canvases stretched over light wood frames. She gave them only a fleeting glance, because it was the walls that drew her eyes. Paintings, framed and unframed, small and large, all in deep, rich colors, hung below the high windows on all four walls. Some were of people, others of places: a busy street, a doorway, children on swings, a bright little streetcar.

She said, "He really does paint, doesn't he?"

"This is nothing," Toni said. "He has stacks of paintings in the garage. Not up on the walls, of course. Just stored neatly so nothing happens to them."

"Does he ever sell them?"

"I guess so. He has to live on something."

Monica pointed to a door in the forward wall. "What's over there?"

"That's where he lives." Toni pushed open the door and let her look. "Isn't this neat?"

It was. Where there were no windows, the walls were filled with bookshelves, and the shelves were filled with books. A narrow bed, covered by a brown-and-beige woven blanket, was under one of the front windows, and under the other was a small table and two chairs. In the corner beyond the table there was a sink, a small refrigerator, and a table-top stove. A couple of brown wicker chairs with beige cushions and two colorful throw rugs completed the furniture.

"You keep it looking nice," Monica said.

"Not just me. He's a neat person." Toni grinned. "In all sorts of ways. Come on," she said, pulling the door closed, "let me show you 'Springtime.'" She stopped to pick up some pencil sketches that were lying on the floor by the worktable. "That Sopa," she muttered. "She's probably smeared these completely." She placed the papers on the table.

Monica followed her across the studio to a corner behind the largest easel. A couple of stacks of paintings leaned against the wall.

"I don't usually mess around this corner," Toni said, "but this is where Sopa was hiding, so I had to move things."

"It does smell sort of funny."

"It stinks," Toni said. "But, remember, she was in here for days. I cleaned up the mess while I was waiting for her to get friendly. And you know how soon that happened." As she talked, Toni pulled a painting out from behind the others and positioned it to face them.

It was a portrait of a girl in her teens wearing a long white dress and holding three red roses. The dress was sleeveless; the neckline, cut modestly low, was scalloped. A string of tiny pearls was around her neck, and her hair, light brown and shoulder length, almost hid drop pearl earrings. She was posed in front of pale green shrubbery that had a few just opening white blooms. A tape pressed on the bottom frame said "Springtime."

Monica gasped. "That's me," she said. "But, of course, it isn't."

"Do you see why I flipped when I saw you standing holding the red geraniums against your shirt?"

"It's got to be my mother," Monica said. "Yes, wait! I remember that dress. We've got photographs of her in it. It was some big event like . . . like—"

"Her *quinceañera!* That's what it was, I'll bet! Was her name Cristina?" Monica nodded and Toni went on, "My mother still talks about Cristina's *quinceañera.*"

"I remember now," Monica said. "That was her fifteenth birthday party, with stuff going on at the church in the day-time and then a big dance at night." Monica paused. "You mean your mother lived here then, too?"

"No. My father did. But she was at the party. There aren't many long-time people on this street. Everybody on Lucia comes and goes except the Almayos, the Salcedos, and El Pintor. And now he's gone."

"He'll be back, won't he?"

"I hope so. We'd better go now." Outside, she said, "I'll see you later. I just live down the block. The house with the pots of marigolds."

After Toni left, Monica stayed where she was, staring at the studio. El Pintor. Who was he? And why was everyone worried because he'd been gone for a few days? Of course, it was strange about Sopa. But maybe he'd thought she was outside when he left. At the thought of Sopa she looked around the yard and found her lying under a shrub, peering at her. "I'll bring you some water," she said as she climbed the steps. "Don't go away."

She was in the kitchen filling a heavy ceramic bowl with water when she heard the front door opening. "Hi, Dad," she called and walked into the dining room. "We have a new—" She stopped so suddenly that some of the water spilled over the bowl onto the floor.

Standing in the living room was a young man wearing khaki shorts and a white T-shirt. He was tall and well-built, and as olive-skinned as her father. There was a startled look on his face as he returned her stare.

Monica's hands grew clammy and her throat choked. What is he doing here? What does he want? Anything can happen in this awful place. She flung the bowl at the man in the living room, spattering water on the dining table and chairs and missing him completely.

"Hey, what's that for?" the stranger said. "What's going on? Let me ask who—"

"Get away from me!" Monica cried.

The young man grinned. "Sure. How far?"

Monica felt hot blood fill her face. "I don't care. Just get out. You don't belong here!"

The young man took a long look around the two rooms, then said, "Maybe I don't. Looks like the painting's been done. El Pintor asked me to do the job before the owner took over—"

"El Pintor!" Monica said crossly. "All I hear is 'El Pintor.' Well, the owners have taken over, so you can leave now."

The stranger bent over, picked up the pieces of the bowl, and placed them on the coffee table. "I'm sorry if I scared you," he said, "but I'm really not dangerous." He started for the door.

Monica sighed a sigh of relief. Then, at a sudden thought, shouted, "Not so fast! You have our key!"

He held up the key with his thumb and forefinger. "I do, don't I? It belongs to El Pintor," he said, placing it on a chair cushion. "I'd appreciate it if you'd return it to him." With that he stepped through the door and pulled it closed behind him.

When her father returned, Monica met him at the door with the story of the intruder.

"Well," her father said, "so Mr. Mead was going to have the house painted for us. That was thoughtful."

"Maybe painting wasn't it at all, Dad. Maybe that guy just needed an excuse to get into the house."

"There's no reason why you shouldn't believe that young man, Monica," her dad said quietly. "He had El Pintor's keys, didn't he? That's certainly enough for me."

"Oh, Dad, you trust everybody. What's with this El Pintor, anyway? Who is he?"

"Who is he?" Her father put the packages in his arms down on the seat of one of the living room chairs and turned back to her. "Nobody really knows. Your mother told me that he showed up here one day when she was just a baby."

"Maybe he was a tramp," Monica said. "A . . . a vagrant."

"Maybe. But don't be so quick to judge. There's probably more to his story—and to him."

Thinking of the paintings she had just seen, Monica nodded. "I guess there'd have to be if they let him hang around for more than thirty years." She sat down on the couch. "Okay. So tell me."

He made room on the chair beside his packages, sat, and said, "I don't have much to tell. And what I do came to me second-hand, really third-hand. Because your mother could not have been aware of this at the time it happened. All I heard is that your grandparents felt sorry for him. They let him hang around and eventually move into the garage."

"That wasn't very smart, was it?"

"The way Cristina told it, her parents decided giving Mr. Mead refuge was the smartest thing they ever did." Her father paused and scratched his head. "I don't know," he said thoughtfully. "They didn't exactly let him live with them, but they certainly did the next closest thing. The studio was just a shack then, and they let him have it. Little by little, your grandfather and Mr. Mead built up the old shack into what it is now. And he's been here ever since. Rent-free. No questions asked." He stood up and picked up his packages. "Now you know as much of his history as I do. I can add that he is one of the most trustworthy individuals I've come across. I've always called him Mr. Mead, but to everyone in this neighborhood, he's known as El Pintor."

When her father left, Monica sat staring out of the living room window. Would she ever get used to living here? On the street an ancient pickup truck loaded with well-used household furniture lumbered toward the end of the block. Across the street the little boys with their barking dogs once more hurtled their skateboards up and down the sidewalk. And right beside her house, hidden behind the studio's grape-colored door, lay a troublesome mystery called El Pintor.

Chapter Three

The following morning two boxes of Monica's things from Raeburn School arrived at the house on Lucia, but not before the arrival of a damp gray overhang of clouds that hid the sun. Although Monica knew that the mist would lift and the sun would eventually appear, that knowledge did nothing for her state of mind. The grayness of the morning matched her mood.

She had awakened early, but when she realized where she was, she closed her eyes tightly, willing herself away from this place. In a few moments she opened them slowly and sighed. No, she was not in the dorm at Raeburn. Yes, she was in her old bed, but not in her old room. That room had gone with the sale of their house, and nothing would bring it back.

I hate this place, she thought, I'll always hate it. And I can't complain to Dad about it; he has enough to worry about. Then, lying there feeling miserable, she thought about her dad's car. She shot out of bed. Quickly, she padded into the narrow hallway and into the living room, breathing fast. Would the car still be there? How long could a BMW, unattended, last in this neighborhood? When she looked through the front window, she calmed down. The car was at the curb in front of their house, right where her father had parked it the night before. Except for a blanket of moisture, it was none the worse for a night in the open. Still, her father was so trusting. She gave the car one last look and returned to bed feeling a little bit foolish, but not at all reassured.

At mid-morning, while her dad was working with the dryer, Monica called her friend Jackie on Parkview Place. Jackie's mother answered the phone.

"Monica!" she said. "Jackie and I were wondering when we'd hear from you. We knew you were back in Los Angeles, and Jackie was so eager to see you before she left."

"Jackie's gone? Where to?"

"She's spending the summer in France. One of those special programs Westbriar puts on for the incoming seniors. She'll be devastated that she missed you."

Monica swallowed hard. "I'm sorry, too. But I'll talk to her when she returns." She managed a decent goodbye and then walked into her room. The phone call was a mistake. It had only added to her gloom.

The arrival of her belongings, with her CD player and her laptop computer both in working order, helped to cut into her mood. Now, all she had to do was make things fit. When she finally had the boxes empty and the room somewhat arranged, she decided to take a break and write Courtney the letter she'd promised her.

"Dear Courtney," she wrote:

I'd e-mail you if we were hooked up, but we're
not, so snail mail will have to do. I know you asked
me to tell you all about the barrio right away, what it
looks like, feels like, etc., etc. Actually, the 'etc.' is as
good as anything I can tell you. What this place
looks like is a neighborhood of really small, kind of
old houses where mostly poor people live. What it
feels like is strange and scary, but then I guess all
brand-new unfamiliar places are like that. You probably figure I'm going to go nosing around the way I
did at Raeburn and have a lot to tell you. Not. Not
around here. So I'm no longer Curious Catherine.
You can think of me as Mind-My-Own-Business
Monica from now on.

The very day we got here I met a girl about my age
named Toni. She seems nice and normal. Also I've
been adopted by a not-so-normal cat named Sopa.
(That means 'soup' in Spanish.)

When and if we get a new address, street or e-mail,
I'll let you know. Write me. Already I'm starving for
news from the outside world.

Maybe writing the letter helped, because by lunch time
she was feeling better. Besides, the sun was out and she had
managed to get all her clothes in the closet. Feeling better,
however, lasted only until just after lunch, because it was
then that her father said, "Monica, I have to be gone for a
few days starting tomorrow. I'm flying to San Francisco."

"Gone? But we just got here."

"That can't be helped. These contacts up there are important."

She picked up their dishes and was rinsing them at the sink to hide her rising tears. "Is there any reason why I can't go with you?" she said.

"A couple."

"I should have known. It's the expense, isn't it?"

"Not just expense. I need my mind clear for business, and I'd be worrying about you. I don't want you roaming around San Francisco on your own."

She swung around, her back to the sink. "But you won't worry if I stay here alone?"

"No more than when you were at Raeburn," he said. Then, when she started to speak, "Hold it, hold it. You won't be alone. When I made those appointments, I thought Mr. Mead would keep an eye on you, but since he's gone, I've asked Laurita Salcedo to stay with you."

"Come on, Dad. I don't need a babysitter."

"Nor is Laurita one. Consider her a companion, or a guest, if you will. Just somebody to keep you from feeling lonely."

Monica gave him a long, thoughtful look. Why did she sense a grin beneath her dad's words? "Laurita Salcedo," she said with a frown of concentration. "Salcedo? Like the guitar shop?"

He nodded. "She and your mother were close friends. Laurita came to our wedding, and she helped nurse your mother in the weeks before she died. I don't know what I would have done without her."

"I don't remember her at all."

"You were pretty small. She's a nice person. I think you'll like her."

"Can't Rosa come?"

"We've already imposed enough on Rosa. Remember, she has a full-time job. Laurita's at loose ends. She lives with her brother's family, and now that the Salcedo kids are grown, there's not much for an old-maid aunt to do."

Monica grimaced. "There won't be anything for her to do here either. She'll probably do nothing but sit and pray. I hope she doesn't click her rosary beads at night."

Now her father did grin. "I hope not. I think you'll find you can bear with her for a couple of days."

Monica returned the grin. "Let's make a deal, Dad. I'll put up with this lady for a couple of days if you'll let me drive you to the airport."

"Not on your life. Not to LAX." He held up his car keys. "But you may have to buy groceries. Laurita can point you to the nearest market." He jingled the keys again. "I'll leave these in the box with the house keys."

"What box? Where?"

"The one in the cupboard on the back porch. It's got keys to this house, the studio, the garage, and, now, the car keys."

Her father left early the next morning. Sopa appeared at the back door not five minutes after he had gone. She was dusty. A couple of ragged cobwebs clung to her fur, but otherwise she seemed all right. "So you're back," Monica said. "Figured you'd better get back before your favorite stuff was all gone, huh?" She scratched the cat behind the ears and brought out a cup of soup. She was still pouring it into Sopa's dish when she heard a shaky metallic rattle coming from the street, then the squeal of brakes, and, above the slamming of car doors, the clamor of children's voices.

Curiosity took her along the side of the house to the front. A battered Volkswagen was parked at the curb by the lamppost, its bumper nudging the BMW. Standing by the little car was a tall, slim woman wearing faded blue jeans and a knit shirt. She had the blackest hair Monica had ever seen. It was cut short, almost like a boy's, with thick, uneven bangs brushed carelessly across her forehead. The woman was surrounded by a group of little boys whom Monica recognized as the ball players.

The big-eared one yanked at his red baseball cap so that its bill sat firmly behind his neck and said, "Man, you call that a ride? Half a block?"

"*¡Bastante, bastante!*" the woman said. "Enough. I warned you I wasn't going far."

"Yeah," another boy said with a grin, "but we didn't believe you."

"And whose problem is that, eh?" the woman countered.

"What'cha gonna do here, Laurita?" Red Cap asked. "You gonna live here?"

"For a few days, César. Now, go on, all of you. Go do whatever you were doing." The woman's eyes went beyond the boys to where Monica stood at the corner of the house. "*No es posible,*" she said, shaking her head and smiling. "You can't be Monica. They must've cloned Cristina."

Monica smiled, too. "I didn't know how much I looked like her until I saw the—" She broke off, not sure if she should mention the painting. "But I'm Monica, all right, and you must be Laurita."

"I confess," the woman said. And then, glancing at the cup that was dangling from Monica's hand, she said, "But I interrupted your coffee. I hope it's not all gone."

"This wasn't coffee. It was soup. For the cat. But there's coffee in the kitchen, if you'll show me how to make it."

"That sounds fair. I'll just get my things." In a moment Laurita appeared at the back door. "Where do I go?" she asked, and Monica showed her to the small back bedroom that had been cleared for her.

Laurita stood under the darkened brass light fixture and looked around the room. "This used to be Chita's, your grandmother's, sewing room," she said. "Over there by the windows was the big power sewing machine where she worked. Piece work from a factory that made ladies' coats and suits."

"Here? She worked here? Why?"

"To support herself and your mother. And your grandfather, too, after his accident. They were such good people. I guess the good do die young, too young, at any rate, for you to have known them."

"Dad says they were still alive when my mother died."

"Only your grandfather. Chita was gone before you were born."

"I guess there aren't many long-life genes in my mother's side of the family."

"It looks that way," Laurita said, running her fingers through her unruly bangs. "But you may have a surprise or two in store for you." She turned to the door. "Can I see the rest of the house?"

They went down the hall to an open door. "This is my room. Dad says it was my mother's room, too."

"It was. I spent many a night here. But it was never as pretty as this." Laurita picked up a green cushion that was shaped like a frog, patted it, and returned it to the bed. Her eyes seemed to twinkle as she looked toward the closet. "Have you found the secret trapdoor yet?"

"Trapdoor? Is there one? Where?"

"In the closet ceiling. Actually, it's just an opening to the crawl space below the roof, but it was too small for anyone but Cristina and me to get through, so it became our place. We liked to call it a trapdoor, even though it wasn't." Laurita's face was flushed with something like excitement that made her look a lot younger. As if to return to the present, she added, "That opening is only big enough for little kids. You have to wonder what the builders were thinking of when they put up these old houses."

"What did you and my mom do up there?"

"Nothing much. It was dark, and, besides, neither one of us liked the idea of spiders. What we did was hide our most secret belongings there."

Monica laughed. "I kept my secret things in a locked box underneath my bed, but I'm sure Rosa knew all along they were there. You don't suppose some of my mother's things could still be up there?"

"I'm not even sure the trapdoor's still there."

"Let's see." Monica stepped inside the closet and looked up. In the ceiling right above her was a barely discernible square outline. "Look," she said, and Laurita squeezed into the closet with her.

"Too bad," Laurita said. "It's been painted over. Two or three times."

"Maybe if we pushed hard with a mop or a broom handle, it would move."

"Maybe," Laurita answered. "But remember this house is old. We don't want to bring down the whole ceiling."

"I've got the knife Dad lent me to open up my cartons. If we used it to cut along the edges, that might loosen it."

"Maybe," Laurita said again, "but I'm not sure it's such a good idea. In any case, I'd better back out, out of the closet and of your trapdoor project, too. Come on, let's go look at the rest of the house."

A tour of the rest of the house took only a couple of minutes. Where they spent their time was outside in the backyard.

When they returned to the kitchen, Laurita measured coffee into a coffee maker and said, "Nothing's changed much except that the poor old lemon tree looks like it hasn't had a drink for months. Every summer, when we were kids, your mother and I picked its lemons and made gallons of lemonade that we sold out front. Movie money. I guess I owe it something. Do you mind if I water it?"

"Of course not. But I don't know if we have a hose. And if we do, it's not in the garage. The garage belongs to the man in the studio."

"El Pintor," Laurita said, "and he's gone. *Bueno, bueno,* after I have my coffee, let's go out in back and see what we can find."

They found a lean-to behind the garage that held garden tools, a hose, and a sturdy stepladder. Monica stared at the ladder and realized all of a sudden that she had made a decision a while back without even knowing it. With or without Laurita's help, she was going to pry open the little door in her closet ceiling. Maybe there, in the place where her mother had stored her closest thoughts and her secrets, maybe there she would feel a sense of her. If there was any good to come out of having to live in this house, it might be getting to know something about her mother. She needed more than the only vision of her that she had, the one where she was always walking gracefully across a garden, her voice as sweet as wind chimes.

Laurita said, "These must be El Pintor's things. How about it, Monica? If we water his flower beds, I think it's all right to use his things, don't you?"

Monica agreed. Later, it occurred to her that she must have agreed to more than watering. Of course, it had all started with the plan to water the lemon tree. But Laurita's enthusiastic approach to work was contagious, and soon they were cutting back geraniums, weeding dried-up flower beds, and raking what someday, according to Laurita, could become a green patch of grass, if watered. They paused midway in their labors to eat tuna sandwiches on the back steps. Sopa, apparently hearing the back door and smelling the tuna, appeared on the side fence, took a few dainty ballet steps along its top edge, leaped to the ground, and started for the back stairs. Halfway there, she stopped. She stared at Laurita for a few thoughtful moments, then turned and padded leisurely the full length of the yard, disappearing behind the garage.

Laurita said, "That's El Pintor's cat, isn't it?"

"Right. I'm taking care of her until he returns—if he ever does."

Laurita took another bite of her sandwich, chewed it as she stared beyond Monica to the studio. "He will. This is the wrong time for him to be gone."

Monica looked at her curiously. "Why do you say that?"

"Just a feeling." Laurita got up and started collecting the remnants of their lunch. In a few minutes they were in the house, flipping a coin to see who would get first chance at the shower.

"*¿Cómo no?*" Laurita said, seeing that she had won. "After all, I'm the dirtiest."

As soon as the bathroom door closed, Monica raced to the shed behind the garage and brought in the stepladder. In the hallway, she paused at the bathroom door. "Did you find towels?" she called.

"Yes. I won't be long, but first I've got to scrape the dirt from under my fingernails."

"Take your time," Monica said and carried the ladder into her bedroom.

She eased it into the closet. It took only a few minutes to cut through the paint along the edges of the four sides of the opening in the ceiling. She had a few rough moments when she hit something metallic with her dad's knife and thought the wooden cover was nailed shut. A bit of scraping showed her that she had run into hinges, and she let out her breath. She paused for a moment, listening. The water was still running in the bathroom. Good. She pushed at the wooden square. It did not move. She gave the edges of the cover several blows with the heel of her hand. Nothing. In a matter of seconds, she was down from the ladder, out onto the back porch, and back with a long-handled sponge mop. Now. She set her feet firmly and gave a sharp push with the mop. There was a small creaking sound as more paint cracked along the edges of the square. Another blow with the long-handled mop. More creaking. She took a deep breath, steadied herself, and gave the wooden cover a stronger blow. There was a sharp crack, a quick complaining whine from the hinges, and a shower of paint scraps and dust as the little door flew open.

Monica gasped, sneezed, and stepped out of the cramped closet. As she did, she heard the water go off in the bathroom. She waited, wondering if Laurita had heard her.

"I'll be out of here in a minute," Laurita called through the bathroom door.

Monica, returning the mop to the back porch, yelled, "No hurry," and congratulated herself on her timing. Now, all I have to do, she thought, is wait until bedtime. But no! Bedtime's such a long way off! In that instant, a decision was made. While Laurita was in the back bedroom dressing, Monica locked the door to her bedroom, and, flashlight in hand, climbed up the stepladder to the open trapdoor.

Chapter Four

It was dark up there. Monica stepped up on the next rung of the stepladder and turned on the flashlight. Before she went any farther, she wanted to see what she was getting into. One more rung and her head and shoulders were through the opening in the closet ceiling. She sent the flashlight beam around the dark space slowly.

It was truly a crawl space, the roof pressing down on the attic floor. Head room, she thought, only for a Lilliputian, or a small army of Lilliputians. The floor of the crawl space was covered with a thick carpet of fine black dirt, and every corner and roof beam was draped with ragged clouds of cobwebs. And, as far as she could see, there was nothing else.

So Laurita's guess was right, she thought. There's nothing of my mother's here. Feeling a mixture of disappointment and relief, she reached for the hinged door, ready to close it, the beam of her flashlight searching for possible spiders. That was when she saw it: a can pushed into a corner where the slanting roof line met the ceiling, a corner just beyond the door's outer edge.

It was a round, red can about eight inches tall. Even though it was almost concealed by a cloak of cobwebs, she recognized what it was. An old-fashioned two-pound coffee can, the kind that trendy restaurants displayed along with old-fashioned coffee grinders and ancient spice racks. If she climbed one more rung, she could stretch her arm over the hinged door and reach it. She shuddered at the thought of her fingers pushing through the sticky webs and maybe awakening a sleeping black widow spider. Still, she had to look in that can, just in case. She stood still for a moment, wondering what to do, then she grinned.

She would make one of her roommate Courtney's "reaching-for" tools. Courtney, who was barely five feet tall, had straightened up a wire hanger, curved its end, and was able to pull things down from the closet shelves and tall bookcases at Raeburn with unbelievable ease. In a matter of minutes, Monica, too, had shaped a wire hanger and had dragged the coffee can to where she could reach it. She dusted it with a paper towel and was out of the closet and on her bedroom floor, ready to lift the lid.

But she was too excited to move. Printed on the lid below a roughly drawn skull and crossbones, was,

Do Not Touch! Property of Cristina Salas

Monica knew there were things inside it, things with bulk and substance. She had felt them shift when she was dusting it. For a few minutes she sat and stared at the rusting red can.

Her mother—how long ago?—had hidden it away. When Monica finally attempted to remove the lid, she found it wouldn't budge. She struggled with it for a few minutes and then resorted to hitting the overlapping side of the lid with a paperweight from her desk, careful not to dent the can. Gently, gently, she tapped the lid and at last it moved, making a scratchy metal-on-metal sound that made her cringe.

Now. She pulled off the lid. A faint, musty scent, sweet and flower-like, rose from the opened container. It was easy to see why. Dry rose petals, curling and brown, lay on and around the three items stored in the can: a small green notebook, a collection of cards, and a thick sealed envelope. Monica dragged out the notebook. Inside its cover was written in a small firm hand, "Property of Cristina Salas, 1465 Lucia Street, Los Angeles, California, U.S.A."

"These are my mother's things," Monica whispered, and felt the skin on her arms turn to goose flesh. The notebook was an address book, one that had comments written beneath the names and addresses. Under Mario Avila was written, "He's cute and nice and I think he likes me. But Laurita's crazy about him, so I won't even smile at him anymore." Quickly, Monica turned to the letter S. There were three listings. First, Luisa Sanchez, with the comment, "Thinks she's more important than our whole class put together." Next, Cheryl Smith. "I think we're going to be friends." Finally, Laurita Salcedo. "My very best friend. She is so good to me. But I guess she's good to everybody."

Monica put the book down and picked up the stack of cards that was held by a disintegrating rubber band. She brushed the dry bits of rubber aside and glanced quickly at the cards. There were some valentines, a few birthday greetings, and one get-well card. She would look at these later, too. What interested her was the last thing in the coffee can, the long envelope that at one time must have been white, but was now yellowed and browning at the edges. It was addressed in a bold, flowing hand. It said, "For Cristina Salas, to be opened only upon the death of her parents." Below that was a signature, "Francis Mead," and a February date. It had been written thirty years earlier. In the lower right-hand corner of the envelope, in the tiny hand Monica now recognized as her mother's, was a note. "I promised El Pintor and I will keep my promise. I won't even tell Laurita about this. And, of course, I can't tell Mamá or Papá."

Why, Monica wondered, why couldn't she tell her parents? The answer was immediate and clear. Of course. If El Pintor had wanted them to know about what was in the envelope, he would have told them. But he had not done that. Instead he had given Cristina a sealed envelope to hold in trust. The thought of her mother, a twelve- or thirteen-year-old girl, stealing into the attic to hide securely the envelope her friend El Pintor had given her, moved Monica deeply. She was moved even more by the thought that her mother had never learned what the envelope held. Her chest tightened, and she blinked back the tears that welled up in her eyes.

She remembered vaguely—or had it been told to her?—
visits with her father to see an old white-haired man in a
wheelchair. The visits had been to a hospital, or a place like
a hospital. She knew now that the old man was her grandfather and that, according to Rosa, he had died of a great sadness, the sadness of losing both his daughter and his wife.
Monica leaned against the side of the bed, staring through
the remaining wetness in her eyes at the envelope in her
hands. Her mother had kept the promise she had made to El
Pintor. She had died before her parents, and the envelope
was still intact.

Almost intact, Monica thought, for as she turned the
envelope over in her hands, she discovered a section the size
of a large paper clip torn from its back. Parts of two handwritten lines showed through the tear. Just a few words, but
those words were enough to make her sit up abruptly. The
top line showed, ". . . better life . . . ," and below that, " . . .
our sec . . ." S, e, c? That had to be the start of "secret." She
lifted the torn edge a little, and a bit of the dry paper fell
away. Yes, the word was secret. Her mouth was dry with
excitement. I have to find out what was so secret. But that
means reading the letter, and should I? I suppose I should
wait and ask Dad. Or, better yet, El Pintor.

Yes, he was the one to ask. But he wasn't around, and
who knew when he'd be coming back. So why should she
wait? If he had wanted Cristina to know what was in the letter, why not Cristina's daughter? Of course, she should see
it. As suddenly as she had that thought, another elbowed its

way through. If her mother, who must have been as curious as she was, or even more so, had kept a promise, maybe she should keep that promise, too. Yes. She would not open the envelope until she asked El Pintor's permission. And she would not tell anyone about it. Not Laurita. Not her father. She returned the envelope to the can, put the lid on tightly, and slid it to a far corner under her bed.

Later, when she and Laurita were having supper, Laurita asked, "Well, Monica, did you find anything?"

Monica looked up sharply into Laurita's smiling eyes. "How did you know?" she asked. "How did you know what I was doing?"

"Because, although you've never been my age, I've been yours," Laurita answered, her smile broadening. "At your age I would've been up on that stepladder the first chance I got. So, what did you find?"

"Some cards," Monica said easily. She had practiced this answer, knowing that it would be a half-truth, just in case. "And an address book you'll want to see."

They spent the evening going through the address book.

"Mario Ávila," Laurita said just before they went to bed. "Cristina could have had him. I didn't want him, even if all the girls fell for him. He was a spiffy dresser, lots of neat plaid shirts, but he was a jerk. *Aunque el mono se vista de seda, mono se queda.*"

"What does that mean?"

Laurita gave her a look of swift surprise. "Don't you know Spanish?"

"Sure I do." Monica hoped her face wasn't as red as it felt. "It's just that . . . just that I don't use it too much. My father insisted I speak it even though none of my friends did."

"Well, then, you're one step ahead of them, aren't you? As for the saying, it doesn't sound as good in English, but it means that even if a monkey dresses in silk, he's still a monkey."

"*Gracias,*" Monica mumbled, and they said goodnight.

Her sleep that night was dotted with dreams. All of the dreams were uncomfortable. In one of them she pushed a tiny Courtney into a coffee can, yelling, "I won't let you out until you learn to talk Spanish!" In another, she and Laurita dug a deep hole in the backyard and dragged from it a frail, whiskered man who was El Pintor. All in all, Monica was glad to awaken and find that it was morning. She sat up in bed and sniffed. Coffee and other good smells. Laurita must be making breakfast. She swung out of bed and called down the hall, "Am I in time for some of that good stuff?"

"Just in time," Laurita called back. "I'll start the eggs."

Breakfast was barely over when there was a knock at the back door. It was Toni, wondering, she said, how Monica was getting along with Sopa and wondering, too, if she had seen El Pintor.

"No," Monica said, glancing eagerly at the studio. "Is he back?"

Toni shrugged. "I guess not, but I was hoping."

"Are you still worried about him?"

"I wasn't," Toni said. "El Pintor's a pretty independent old guy." She wrinkled up her nose in something like a frown, shook her head, and sat down on a porch step. "Then Roberto came home, and he's fit to be tied about El Pintor."

"Who's Roberto?"

"My brother. He just got back from college. And the first person he wanted to see was El Pintor." Toni rolled her eyes to the sky. "You should've heard the explosion when we told him how long El Pintor's been gone."

"Does he think something's wrong?"

"I don't know. I tuned him out after a while. El Pintor's done a lot for him, an awful lot. My mother swears El Pintor's a saint. Maybe he is. As far as I'm concerned, he's just a nice old guy, and I sure wish he'd come home."

"I do, too," Monica said softly. The sound of the words surprised her. She hadn't meant to say them. Then her eye caught a movement at the corner of the house. Rounding the corner of the house, wearing old sneakers, khaki shorts, and another white T-shirt, was the same guy she'd found in her living room two days before. She jumped up. "Hey, you! What're you doing here again?"

Toni stood up slowly. There was a smile on her lips, a twinkle in her eye. "You're pretty sneaky, aren't you, Rob?

I know I'm just your sister, but you might have said that you knew Monica."

Rob shrugged. "Sorry. I forgot."

"Well, *I* didn't," Monica said. "You scared the life out of me. Do you always sneak up on people?"

"What're you two talking about?" Toni demanded.

"The other day he—" Monica started, but Rob interrupted.

"It's about El Pintor," he said stridently. "And the job he had laid out for me. He wanted me to paint the Ramos house; he'd mailed me the key. So I went to check the place out. How'd I know it had already been painted and that it was occupied?"

Toni had an impish grin on her face as she said, "If that's the case, what're you doing back here again?"

Rob glared at her. "Looking for you. Do you have the key to the studio?"

"Yes, but I don't think—"

"I know what you don't think," Rob shot back. "But I think we have to do it. Where else can we find out what's happened to El Pintor?"

"I don't know," Toni said, shaking her head slowly. "Honestly, Rob, I don't know what to do."

"I think you should let him," Monica said in a quiet voice. Toni spun around, her face showing surprise. "What harm can it do? You let me see 'Springtime.' Anyway, he's right. There's nowhere else, is there, where you can get a hint of what was going on with El Pintor before he disappeared?"

"I guess not." Toni went down the porch steps. "All right, Rob, but please make it fast and don't move things around too much."

"Relax, little sister," Rob said. To Monica he called out, "Thanks."

"No big deal," Monica answered. "I'd like to see you find him, too. I'd kind of like to meet him."

"He's an impressive man. Come on, Toni, let's get started."

Monica felt left out as she watched them enter the studio. And why? After all, she told herself, this is really none of my business. I don't even know El Pintor. But he did write that letter to my mother that I just *have* to read and that I can't until I get his permission. Her thoughts were interrupted when the boy in the red cap, the one called César, came racing around the side of the house.

"Where's Sopa?" he asked, panting. "I've been chasing her and I saw her come in here."

"Chasing her? Why?"

"*Why?*" The little boy threw his arms out and looked at her with disdain. "Jeez! For El Pintor, of course. She was way out at the other end of the street. He'll think he's lost her."

"No, he won't. Cats roam all over the place. Anyway, El Pintor's not back. He's the one who's lost."

The boy called César stamped his foot. "Don't say that!" he yelled.

She looked down from where she stood on the steps at his angry face that was pinched and coloring and truly wished that she hadn't said what she had. "I'm sorry," she said. "But don't worry, Roberto's going to look for him. And he'll find him."

César shot a funny little look up at her. "How would you know? You don't know where he went or where he is. And somebody oughtta know."

Suddenly he began to cry.

Monica was searching her mind for something reassuring to say when César spun around and, with a quick swipe of his arm across his eyes, fled around the corner of the house.

Chapter Five

After César left, Monica remained on the back porch stoop, staring blankly at the studio door. She knew she should do the dishes she'd promised Laurita she would do, but something was holding her outside. It was pleasant sitting on the steps. The sun had broken through the gray mist early and was now washing the backyard with a soft, golden light. But I'm not sitting here because it's such a pleasant morning, she told herself; I'm sitting here because of the studio. Her eyes had not left its door, and now she knew why.

There was something in the studio that she needed to see again. What it was she didn't know. She knew only that whatever it was, it had made an impression, an impression that was instantly forgotten when she had caught sight of "Springtime." *What was it?* She had to get into the studio to find out.

With her mind made up, she hurried down the porch steps, but at the bottom she paused, her hand hesitating on the wooden railing. This was not the right time, not with two other people going through the cupboards and closets and El Pintor's papers. She needed a few quiet moments to look carefully at everything she had seen in there before: the walls hung with finished paintings; the easels with works in progress; the worktable scattered with sketch pads, pencils and brushes; the living area with all those books and brightly colored little rugs. Whatever had impressed her had done so with only a casual look. Maybe it had nothing to do with El Pintor or El Pintor's being gone, but she had to know. And there was only one way to know: discover what had caught her attention.

Monica glanced at the closed studio door. When Toni and Rob came out, there might be an opportunity for her to go in. She settled herself on the bottom step to wait. Meanwhile, she would try to figure a logical reason for going into the studio, one that Toni might buy.

A bright flash of blue in the far corner of the yard caught her eye. A bird, a blue jay, had swooped suddenly toward the low-growing branches of a large bush. Another jay joined the first, squawking and scolding as it, too, dived and circled near the ground. She soon saw the reason for the commotion. Sopa lay serenely curled up under the bush, showing no concern for the chaos she was causing. She threw the jays a sympathetic glance, thinking that they must have a nest nearby, and then returned to her own problem. Almost immediately, she found the answer to her dilemma. An obvious, easy answer. Wasn't it only two days before that her father had told her there was a key to the studio in the box in the back porch cupboard?

Now, more relaxed, she decided that her next step was to wait for Toni and Rob and discover what they might have found. Meanwhile, she watched the blue jays' attempts to dislodge Sopa from under the bush. Before long, their efforts were rewarded. Sopa rose leisurely, her colorful coat glistening in the morning sunlight, and padded nonchalantly to the back of the garage. In a matter of minutes, Toni and Rob appeared.

"I told you there'd be nothing there," Toni was saying as they came out of the studio. "We didn't learn a thing."

"You're wrong," Rob said, shaking his head. "We learned a lot. We learned that whatever happened to El Pintor, it was something unexpected. None of his clothes are gone. That old suitcase of his is still on the shelf. One of his brushes was waiting to be cleaned. And, along with the fact that he'd left Sopa inside, we can be damn sure he was planning to be back that day."

Toni shrugged. "So? Where does that leave us?"

"I'm not sure," he answered. "One step ahead of where we were before, anyway." His eyes went beyond Toni to where Monica was sitting. "Hi again," he called. And then, "My name's Rob, or Roberto, if you want. What should I call you?"

"My name's Monica. Try that."

"Monica. Right. Well, Monica, I have a favor to ask of you. If you see anything, or hear anything about El Pintor, will you let me know? Maybe some mail will be delivered to your house for him or somebody might come looking for him. Anything. Anything at all."

"Okay, but up to now it's just you guys and that little boy called César who've asked about him. That little kid was really upset. He even started to cry."

Rob said, "I'll go talk to him." He went off between the houses toward the street with Toni beside him.

Inside, Monica checked the key box. She picked out the studio key and slipped it into the pocket of her denim shorts. As soon as she did the breakfast dishes, she would go next door and start her search. But it was mid-afternoon before she finally found herself in the studio. Events, beginning with a telephone call from her father, conspired against her.

"My hands are wet, Laurita," she called from the kitchen when she heard the ringing. "Will you get the phone?"

When Laurita told her who was calling, she hurried to the telephone stand in the hall. "Hi, Dad," she said. "When are you coming back?" An apologetic note in his quick greeting gave her her answer. Not soon. Her father, she learned, needed to stay in San Francisco for another few days. Things were going remarkably well for him, he said, and he felt he should stay with it.

"Even over the weekend?" she asked.

"Weekends are sometimes the best times for contacts, honey. Picture me at a couple of dinner parties, bringing out the charm." He went on to say that he had already made tentative arrangements for Laurita to stay with her. All that was needed was Monica's approval.

She gave it, trying to keep the reluctance out of her voice. She cradled the phone, not knowing what to feel: gladness that things were going well for him or anger at being left on her own in a neighborhood that might as well have been a foreign land.

Back in the kitchen, she found Laurita standing by the open refrigerator door. "Looks like it's time to buy groceries," she said. "It's pretty empty."

"Now?" Monica asked, dismayed.

"Why not?"

Because I want to look around the studio right away, she thought, but said, "Okay. Let's get it over with. So long as I can drive the Beemer."

"Beemer?"

"My dad's BMW. I don't often get to drive it."

"If you have the keys and your dad's permission, let's go."

They made quick work of the grocery shopping. As they got into the car, Laurita said, *"Teniendo caballo ensillado, se encuentra mandado.* Would you mind a quick stop at the guitar shop?"

"No problem. But what did you say about a horse?" Something about a horse and finding something."

"It's a *dicho,* Monica. A saying. 'If you have a saddled horse, you're sure to find an errand.'"

"Cool," Monica said with a grin. "I suppose I'm the horse."

In just a few minutes, they were turning into the parking area behind the Salcedos' small building. Two of the six parking spaces were taken up by a glossy green van, "Salcedo's Guitars" printed on its doors, and a dusty pickup truck. Monica pulled her dad's car into one of the narrow slots, and they went into the shop through a screened back door.

The room they entered was obviously a workshop, with the sweet smell of wood and wood polishes heavy in the air. The walls were hung with what looked like patterns for guitars and guitars at several stages of completion, all of them different. Two men, both wearing stained white T-shirts, were at work at large wooden tables. One, a thin middle-aged man with an abundance of laugh lines on either side of his dark eyes, reminded Monica of her father. The other man was young. He had a shock of unruly black hair over a face that was long and angular. A wide, sensitive mouth softened the stubborn line of his chin. He bent more deeply over his work as they walked in.

"*Hola, hombres,*" Laurita said cheerily. "*¿Qué va?*"

"The usual," the older man answered in English. "Push, push, push, to get the orders completed. Every customer wants his guitar to sound as if a choir of angels put it together, and he wants it ready now."

"They'll wait," Laurita said. They know you make the sweetest guitars in California." She turned to Monica. "Monica, this surly fellow is my brother Pancho and the quiet one is his son, my nephew José."

"I'm glad to meet both of you. Thanks for lending Laurita to us."

"You're welcome to her," Pancho said with a grin. "But may we borrow her back this afternoon? My wife has to go to a funeral, and we need someone out front."

"Monica?" Laurita asked.

"Sure," Monica said. Good. Now she wouldn't have to explain her visit to the studio.

Laurita left for the guitar shop right after lunch. Not five minutes after that, Monica was at the studio door.

Inside, she stood with her back against the door, still grasping the doorknob, her heart racing foolishly. She took several deep breaths, and told herself that she was not here to commit a robbery, and, if she was trespassing, it wasn't all that bad because didn't her dad and she own the property? She knew she was rationalizing, but, even so, that thinking reassured her, and she took a few steps into the room. There she made a quick turn, glancing at everything just as she had on that first day. Then she slowed down and looked, one by one, at the bright paintings hung high on the wall. She stared for a moment at the one of a small orange-red streetcar and drew in her breath as she realized that this painting was familiar. It was the little streetcar that went up and down Angels' Flight in downtown Los Angeles. She remembered reading that it had been dug out of storage, reconditioned, and replaced in a spot close by its original location. Was that what had caught her eye? It might have been, but something told her, no. Whatever she had seen had touched her in a different way. Not just for its familiarity but because . . . because . . . because *what?*

I have to do this systematically, she told herself, and moved quickly into the small front room where El Pintor ate and slept. And read, she thought, as she contemplated the shelves of books. She started to take one down and stopped. She hadn't touched anything that other time; of that she was sure. Had Toni? She closed her eyes, remembering. Yes, Toni had moved all the paintings that were stacked in front of "Springtime." Maybe that's where she had caught a glimpse of whatever it was. But hold it. Toni had moved something else. There had been three or four pencil sketches lying on the floor by the worktable in the other room, and Toni had scooped them up and, complaining about Sopa's treatment of them, had placed them on top of the table.

Monica closed the door to the living area and went directly to the worktable. Everything was as she had seen it before: brushes upended in a jar, pencils in another, and sketch pads stacked neatly. She closed her eyes again. The remembered scene appeared as quickly as a Polaroid snapshot. Toni, in her white shorts and blue shirt, bending over to retrieve the pictures and then placing them idly on the table. "Come on," she had said then, "let me show you 'Springtime.'"

The drawings had been lying loose on the table, Monica was sure of that. They weren't there now. So, when Rob and Toni were here earlier today, Toni, tidying up after her brother, must have slipped them into one of the sketch pads. Monica leaned over the table and pulled the top pad toward her.

As she did, three loose drawings slipped onto the table top from between the stack of pads. Monica held back a gasp as she glanced at them. No wonder they had made an impression. She picked up the drawing that was closest to her. It was of an old-fashioned bandstand bordered by shrubs and trees. A church's bell tower showed above the trees. She had heard that bell ring many times as it chimed the hours. The bell tower belonged to the church across the street from St. Francis Park, and St. Francis Park had belonged to the neighborhood kids. She had spent many hours playing there.

She placed the other two pictures side by side, and this time she did gasp. The first drawing was of an old man and a little girl standing by an ice-cream truck labeled "Dan, the Ice-Cream Man." She knew those two people. The girl was Jana, her little neighbor on Parkview Place. But not so little as she remembered her. In this drawing, Jana was half a head taller than when Monica had visited her neighbors the previous summer. The man was Mr. Daniels, who had been selling ice cream from his truck to the kids on Parkview for as long as she could remember. Sketched in the background was the house she had been born in and lived in until her dad and she had gone to Washington. She stared at the picture as a chill covered her arms with goose bumps. This was creepy. Eagerly, she turned to the last picture. It was another corner of St. Francis Park, a secluded bench backed by flowering shrubs, with the swings and the slide of the play area showing behind them.

Monica took the three drawings and sat on the floor to study them. There was no question in her mind about the places and the people in these pictures. They were of her street, her house, her neighbor, her neighborhood park. But why? *Why?* She stared at the sketches for ten long minutes. When no answer came, she rose, returned the drawings to the worktable and, frowning, let herself out of the studio.

Chapter Six

Monica clicked off the television set and tossed the remote control unit onto the living room coffee table. "Easy for you," she said to the darkened TV screen. "You people in the soaps can always figure things out. Somebody writes the answers for you."

It was an hour since she had left the studio. In that time nothing had kept her mind off the pencil sketches. There had to be a reason for them, but what? She was aware that El Pintor knew where they had lived—her father had said that he'd come to her mother's funeral—and Toni had said that he went all over the city on buses to do his sketching, but why had he picked her old neighborhood? And why *her* house?

She stepped out on the porch and, leaning against the porch pillar at the top of the steps, looked up and down Lucia. On the other side of the street, on the front steps of the house directly across from her, two women sat talking. As Monica watched, one woman slapped the other on the knee, threw her head back and laughed loudly. Otherwise, the street was strangely calm. No skateboards, no ball games, and only an occasional car coming or going on the asphalt. She went down the steps and stood on the cement walkway that led from the sidewalk to the house. She knew what lay to the west; she had driven that way with her father and also earlier today. But to the east? Several blocks in that direction, maybe half a mile away, there was a rise in the land, a gradual slope that appeared to be covered with greenery, perhaps large shrubs or small trees.

Monica squinted into the distance, wondering if what she saw could be a park. When she realized that she was wondering about something other than the drawings, she knew what she had found to do. A walk. She would go for a walk. Being inside was driving her crazy, and the street looked safe enough. She hurried inside to lock the house and in a few minutes was headed east.

Holding the house key tightly in her hand, Monica walked quickly by the first few houses, then, aware of the tension she was feeling, shoved the key into her shorts pocket and slowed down. For the most part, the windows and doors of the houses she was passing were open, guarded only by screens, and the sounds of laughter and music and of voices calling from room to room mingled in the summer air with the scent of browning garlic and onions and a medley of rich spices. She relaxed. Nothing she saw or heard seemed menacing. After a few blocks the look of the street changed. The houses began to thin out. Empty lots, some with the shattered remains of old foundations, were scattered between them. Close to the curbs there were trees growing whose roots, unlike the pepper trees at the other end of Lucia, pushed up cracked segments of the cement sidewalk and raised thick, knotted fingers of black asphalt in the street.

After stumbling on the uneven sidewalk, Monica tried to watch her steps, but found it hard to do because her eyes were held by the slope ahead of her. What was this place? There were shrubs and trees on it, although scraggly and overgrown. About mid-slope, in a direct line with the center of Lucia, the tops of two cement pillars pushed through a mass of ivy. Showing above the ivy on each pillar was the upper half of a carved cement urn. The mouths of the two urns were gashed and broken, and it was obvious that over the years, birds often had perched on them. Beyond them she saw a few jacaranda trees with clusters of their spring-time foliage, now a fading lavender, still remaining on their branches. She trudged up the slope on an asphalt driveway that was cracked and weed-grown and paused between the pillars. She decided that what she was looking at beyond the trees was the leftover foundation of another old house.

She took a step or two past the pillars and peered through the trees. Yes, there was a low, crumbling wall—obviously a raised foundation—that outlined a large floor plan. It was about two feet high, with broken gaps that the invading ivy filled somewhat. At the far end and on one side were the broken remains of two or three brick chimneys that extended no more than five or six feet above the ground. These, too, were covered with ivy, only a hint of red brick showing here and there through the encroaching green.

A movement above the nearest chimney stack caught Monica's eye. A puff of smoke drifted for a moment over the broken bricks, then was blown away by an idle breeze. A fire in that chimney? No, of course not. But it *was* smoke. She'd caught a whiff of it. It smelled like Veronica's room at Raeburn, where all the potheads gathered. Someone was sitting behind that chimney smoking marijuana. As if to confirm her assumption, another small cloud of smoke rose above the chimney, this time accompanied by the sound of voices and high-pitched laughter. This is no place for me, Monica thought, and swung around, ready to race down the slope. But with the first step she took, her foot caught on a vine, and she went tumbling to the ground. She pushed up to her hands and knees and was about to scramble to her feet, when she heard a voice behind her.

"Well, look who's here, Licha. Little Miss BMW."

Monica rose stiffly. She brushed off her hands and knees and turned. A teenage girl stood there, her thin frame encased in a white T-shirt that was so long only a pencil-slim line of red shorts showed below it. She had small features and a mass of reddish-brown hair that was highlighted on one side by an inch-wide stripe dyed green. Behind her, clambering up from the shelter of the shattered fireplace, was a plump girl wearing jeans and a short striped shirt. She

had straight black hair that hung well below her shoulders, round black eyes, and full lips that were coated with purple lipstick.

Monica recognized the girls. They were the two who earlier had been flirting with the boys as they worked on their car.

"What'cha doing here?" the plump girl said.

"Why, nothing. I was just—"

"She's snooping," the first girl said. "What else?"

"Yeah, she's a spy!" the girl called Licha said.

"One of El Pintor's cops, that's what she is," the other girl said. "And he sent her out to get us!" The two girls burst into fits of giggles. But as suddenly as the giggles started, they stopped. There was a nasty note in the voice of the girl in the outsize T-shirt as she said, "Don't you ever, ever follow us again, do you hear?"

"You tell her, Josie," Licha cried. "Tell her what we'll do to her."

Monica, who had been silent during the outbreak of giggles, now found her voice. "Follow you? I wasn't following you. Why would I want to do that?"

"Go ahead, play dumb," Josie said, "but we know all about El Pintor. It's enough to gag you. What's he trying to do? Pull us into listening to his preaching? Get real."

"Look who needs to get real," Monica said. "Spies. Cops. El Pintor a preacher. What are you two smoking, anyway?"

Josie's face turned red. She clenched her fists as she said, "Get outta here! And if you know what's good for you, you'll forget you saw us." Suddenly, her eyes went beyond Monica, and she hissed, "Jee-ee-eepers kraut! What're you doing here?"

Monica turned. The little boy called César was standing by one of the cement pillars. She took a step toward him, ready to protect him, when she heard him laugh.

"What d'ya think I'm doing?" he said. "I'm listening. And, man, are you two dumb. She doesn't know anything. She doesn't even know El Pintor."

Monica relaxed a little. César, it seemed, could take care of himself.

"Get lost, snotnose," Josie growled. "And I mean now!"

Licha took a few steps toward the boy. "César!" she cried. "Go on. Go on home!"

The little boy leaned against the pillar, and the ivy made soft, cracking sounds as some of the dry stems broke. He pushed his hands into his pockets and sniffed in an exaggerated way. "I smell something," he said with a knowing grin.

Monica, watching the angry girls and the defiant little boy, decided that it was time to act. She went to the boy, took his hand, and said, "Come on, let's go." César held back, but Monica hung on to him.

With his free hand, the boy reached behind his neck and pulled at the beak of his baseball cap, settling it more snugly on his head. He looked up at her, a question on his face. "They ain't gonna rumble," he said. "Not with me. But, okay, I'll go back with you."

As they started down the slope, César glanced over his shoulder, pulled at Monica's arm, and yelled "Duck!" As she did, a solid clod of earth flew over her head, exploding in a cloud of dust and grit a yard or two beyond them. Monica tightened her hold on the boy's hand and raced down to the street.

At the bottom of the slope, César shook her hand away. "You don't have to be scared of them. They're all mouth."

"They sounded pretty mean to me," Monica answered. "Who are they?"

"That's my sister Licha and her dumb friend, Josie. Josie doesn't live on our street. And Papá doesn't like Licha to hang around with her."

"I don't blame him."

César said, "They were smoking dope."

"I know."

"You *did?* How?"

Monica laughed. "Just like you. I smelled it."

"Oh." César looked up, his dark eyes scanning her face appraisingly. They walked silently for a few moments, and then he said, "I gotta go now. That's my house over there."

He raced across the street to a house with a tall tree in its front yard. A tire held by a thick rope hung from a branch of the tree. She watched as he pushed the tire, started it swinging, and then ran up two shallow steps and through his front door. As she came near her own house, Monica glanced at the loose shutter and the dry and cracking paint on the walls with feelings of relief and something close to gladness. The feelings surprised her. She frowned, then shrugged.

Across the street the two women she had seen earlier were still sitting on the front porch steps talking and laughing.

Inside the house, Monica leaned against the closed door and took a deep breath. She was still shaky. She'd been around girls who were bullies before, but here in this barrio Josie and Licha had seemed terribly dangerous. What had she expected? A gun? A knife? She grinned. What she'd gotten was a clump of dirt that missed. They're all mouth, César had said, and he was probably right.

There was one thing to look at, though. Did those two girls have a special connection with El Pintor? From all she'd heard, it sounded as if El Pintor was trying to drill some sense into all the neighborhood kids. And from what she'd seen, it looked as if Josie would have none of it. Maybe it was only Licha that El Pintor was trying to reach. If it was Josie, too, she wished him luck.

It wasn't long until the two girls were gone from Monica's mind. Instead, the questions about El Pintor's pencil drawings were back. El Pintor, she told herself, had not put those drawings away very carefully, or else they wouldn't have been lying on the floor. It made no difference that

Sopa, in her struggles to get outside, might have scattered them on the floor. If they had been inside a folder or a drawer, Sopa couldn't have done that. So, if he hadn't filed them away, didn't that mean that he wasn't through with them? And couldn't that mean that he was planning to do more drawings in that neighborhood? And wasn't it possible that he had gone back there on the day he disappeared? There were the goose bumps again. I think I'm on to something, she thought. If Rob really wants to look for him, Parkview Place is the spot to start.

Now she made a beeline for the telephone. Sitting on the floor, the phone directory on her lap, she turned to the letter A. Almayo. Toni had said her last name was Almayo. She thumbed quickly through the book and sat back dismayed. There were pages of Almayos. But they couldn't all live on Lucia. She sat up and ran her index finger along the addresses. Halfway down the second page, she found a number on Lucia.

And after two rings,Toni answered the phone.

"Toni? This is Monica. Monica Ramos. You know, next door to El Pintor."

"Of course, I know," Toni interrupted. "What's up?"

"I'm not sure, but I think I found something that might be a clue about El Pintor."

"You did? What? What?"

"It would be easier if I showed you. Could you guys come up here for a minute?"

"Oh, crud, I can't."

"You can't? How about your brother?"

"Rob's gone. He took his pickup to help our cousin Al move. Who knows when he'll be back. And my mother is sick, so I'm stuck at home. How about if we come first thing in the morning?"

"Sure," Monica said flatly, "that's fine. In the morning." She cradled the phone and swallowed her disappointment. She had been ready to fly out and find El Pintor.

Chapter Seven

It was the sound of a hundred bees buzzing around her head. No. It was a referee's whistle that kept pealing over and over again. Monica twisted around in bed and pushed her face into her pillow. No. It was neither. She awakened to the telephone that was ringing. She stretched her arm out for the phone on her bedside table, but there was no phone there. And no table. Now Monica was fully awake and aware of where she was. There was only one phone in the house on Lucia, and it was in the hall.

Who would be calling at this time? Her father, of course! There must be something wrong. But the voice that answered her frantic hello was not her father's. It was a man's, and unfamiliar.

"Monica. Sorry to be calling so late, but I couldn't wait."

"Who is this?" Monica said as the light went on in Laurita's room.

"This is Rob, Roberto Almayo. And I've got to know what you found." He paused, then added quickly, "Hey, did I wake you up?"

Hurriedly pulling on a light cotton robe, Laurita was standing in the hall door.

"Yes," Monica said, "I guess I'm still half asleep." She covered the phone with her hand. "It's Roberto Almayo," she said to Laurita. "He wants to talk about El Pintor."

Laurita shook her head and mumbled something that Monica couldn't hear because Rob was speaking. "I guess I've gone and done it again," he was saying. "Never figured you'd be in bed at eleven."

Monica held back her irritation. "A lot of people are in bed by eleven," she said coolly. "Except for owls. You must be an owl. I, for one, am a lark. I'm a morning person."

"Does that mean that I should hang up and let you go back to bed?"

"You might as well. It'll be easier to show you what I found than to try to describe it—and what I think it means—on the phone. Besides, what could you do about it tonight?" The moment those last words were out, she wished she could bite them back. Hadn't she been just as eager as Rob a few hours before?

"Well, then," Rob said awkwardly, "goodnight."

"Before you say goodnight," Monica said quickly, "let me—"

"Before I say goodnight," Rob interrupted, "let me apologize again and ask how early a lark begins to chirp."

"I don't chirp," Monica said with a laugh, "and you can come before breakfast, whenever that is for you." She returned the phone to its cradle.

The light was on in the kitchen. Monica found Laurita there, warming milk in a saucepan on the stove. Laurita indicated the milk and asked, "Want some?"

"Sure." Monica brought out two mugs and placed them on the kitchen table.

They sipped the hot milk silently for a few moments, then Laurita said, "Roberto's still much too impulsive."

"You mean the late phone call."

Laurita nodded.

"That wasn't so bad, really," Monica said. "He's upset about El Pintor, and he knew I'd found—" She stopped abruptly and then decided she might as well tell Laurita the whole story. Maybe, just maybe, she could throw some light on it. "While you were gone today, I went into the studio. I'd seen something there earlier—I didn't know what—that kept bugging me. And when I found what it was, it bugged me even more. But I decided it had to be a clue to where El Pintor was on the day that he disappeared. So I left a message with Toni for Rob. That's why he called me."

Laurita took a sip of milk. Without raising her eyes from the tabletop, she asked, "What did you find there?"

Monica told her about the three drawings, about how weird the whole thing seemed to her, and ended by asking, "Why would he want to draw places in my neighborhood?" As she said that, something occurred to her that had not occurred before. "Holy pajamas! It just dawned on me. It *could* be just a coincidence."

Laurita said, "Stranger things have happened. But I don't think it's a coincidence. He undoubtedly had a reason." She sat back in her chair, her face puckering into a frown. "You know, Monica," she said, "El Pintor was very fond of Cristina. She was as nice as she was pretty, and, after all, he'd watched her grow up."

"My dad says he came here when she was a baby."

"Yes, that's what I've heard, too. El Pintor was her friend. Whenever Cristina was angry at her parents, even when she was wrong, El Pintor was the one that she'd complain to, and he listened. She always had him to run to. I was jealous of that. The only one I could complain to was your mother, and that wasn't the same as an understanding grownup." Laurita sighed. "None of us saw Cristina much after she married, but when El Pintor heard that she was dying, he went and sat by her bedside whenever he could."

"Oh." Monica found it hard to say more. Finally, she cleared her throat and said, "But what does that have to do with the sketches I found?"

"Maybe nothing," Laurita said with a little laugh. "Anyway, why he's been sketching those particular places isn't the point, is it?"

"No," Monica answered. "What we have to figure out is, was that what he was doing on the day he didn't return? And the way I figure it, he was back there again."

Laurita smiled. "We? So you're in it, are you? You want to find him, too. Why?"

Monica was stumped for an answer. She couldn't tell Laurita about the envelope she had found in the attic; she had made a vow to herself to keep her mother's promise as well as her own. Her face was hot. She knew it was turning red. Even as a little kid, her blushing face had betrayed her most innocent white lies. Now she said, "I guess I'm curious. You know, all this mystery . . . and everyone seems to like him so much . . ." She was blathering; she knew that, but she couldn't stop herself. ". . . and Rob is so worried about him, so I just . . . I just decided I ought to help."

Laurita said, "Roberto will need your help." She stood up. "I'll wish you good luck in the morning, but right now I need some sleep."

"Me, too. And something tells me that Rob'll be here early."

He came in time for breakfast. Planned or unplanned, he arrived just as Laurita declared the scrambled eggs done, just as the toast popped up in the toaster, and just as Monica finished filling the glasses with orange juice.

The knocking at the back door was timid, so gentle that Monica and Laurita weren't sure they had really heard it. But when it came again, Monica went to the door and found Rob standing there. His hair was damp and he smelled of soap and after-shave. His white T-shirt was rumpled, half tucked into his plaid shorts, the other half hanging over them as if he had dressed hurriedly.

"I didn't wake you up?" he asked in a hushed voice.

"You don't have to whisper," Monica said. "We're up. Come on in. You're just in time for breakfast."

When Laurita saw him she set another place at the table and said, "Sit down, Roberto."

He accepted the invitation without any hesitation. "This is great," he said. "My mother has one of her migraine headaches—that's why Toni isn't here—and I had to get my own breakfast, so all I had was corn flakes."

"Helpless macho," Laurita muttered and placed a plate of scrambled eggs and bacon before him.

"What? No salsa?" Rob said with a grin and ducked when Laurita flicked his cheek.

"*Limosnero con garrote.* A beggar with a club," she said to Monica, "in case you were going to ask." Rob shrugged and dug into the food on his plate.

When they were through eating, Rob asked to do the dishes to prove he wasn't a "helpless macho," but Laurita shooed them out of the kitchen. So, within minutes, Rob and Monica were standing by the worktable in the studio, the three pencil drawings spread before them.

"I know all these places," Monica began, "and I know the people he drew, too. It's the neighborhood I grew up in." She went on to explain why she thought the pictures might be a clue to El Pintor's whereabouts on the day of his disappearance. Rob listened without interrupting, but as she spoke, a frown grew on his face.

When she was through, he said, "I guess it's worth snooping around there a little bit, but that's a pretty skimpy reason for deciding he was there."

Monica bit back her disappointment. She had been so sure he would agree with her.

"Hey," he said, "I'm not putting your idea down entirely. It's just that why couldn't he have done these last year, or even a month or two ago?"

"Oh, oh, oh," she said eagerly. "I left that out, didn't I? He couldn't have." She pulled the sketch of the ice-cream truck closer. "Look. Last year Jana—that's the little girl— was lots shorter, and her hair was just below her ears. Look, it's below her shoulders now."

"How do you know it's the same little girl?"

She let out her breath in exasperation. "Because it's Jana, that's how. El Pintor did a good likeness. Besides, the T-shirt she's wearing? See the huge sunflower on it? It used to be her sister's. My friend Jackie's."

"Okay, okay, you've made your point. These drawings were done recently, but how recently? They could have been done a couple of months ago, and that wouldn't help at all since El Pintor's only been gone for about a week."

"I give up," Monica said angrily. "I give up completely. You're right, I'm wrong. From what you say, these pictures don't help at all. But, look, if you're so worried about him, why don't you call the police? Sure. Why don't you call the Missing Persons Bureau?"

"Because I'm the only one who's worried. The police wouldn't listen to me. After all, I'm not a relative, and besides, El Pintor has a right to come and go as he pleases. He doesn't have to report to anyone. But I know him and I *am* worried. Look, Monica, these pictures are a good starting place to look for him. I'm sorry if my questions bothered you. I'm just trying to be logical."

"So am I," Monica said crisply, gathering up the pictures. "And these drawings had me pretty convinced." She bent across the table to stack them with the sketch pads. Abruptly, she pulled back and returned them to the tabletop. She picked up the drawing of Jana and the ice-cream truck and held it out to Rob. "And now I know why," she said triumphantly. "Why hadn't I pointed this out to you before? See? It's Mr. Daniels. He never, and I mean *never,* brings his ice-cream truck to our neighborhood before school is out. And the schools there weren't out till last Wednesday. There. How do you like that for pinning down the time? This drawing couldn't have been done before last Thursday or Friday."

"Are you sure—?" Rob caught himself. "Yes, you're sure or you wouldn't look so smug."

"Well, I feel smug. Because I know, on this one, I'm absolutely right. And, besides, it's a very important point." Rob laughed, and, she thought, he's even more handsome when he laughs. I like the way his eyes, all on their own, seem to laugh, too.

Rob handed her the pictures. "If it wasn't for you, I'd have nothing to go on. I honestly don't know how to thank you."

"You don't have to thank me. I didn't snoop around here only for you. I want to find him, too." Rob looked quizzically at her and she added, "I have my reasons."

"In that case, do you want to go with me?"

Monica looked at him with surprise. "Try to go without me," she said.

Chapter Eight

Twenty minutes later, the studio was locked, Laurita had been told where they were going, and Monica was sitting on her front steps waiting for Rob to pick her up. Although it was after nine o'clock, Lucia Street was strangely quiet. What activity there was, was at the far end of the street beyond César's house, where two men were patching a roof. The rapping of their hammers was the only sound that reached her.

Monica's eyes were drawn to the masses of flowers fronting El Pintor's house. Laurita and she had watered them thoroughly, and they seemed to have responded with heightened color. As she stared at the bright flower beds, Monica's thoughts and gaze blurred into a vision, a vision of El Pintor as he stepped out of his grape-colored door on that day last week when he had not returned.

In her mind's eye he wore a loose, almost baggy, gray cardigan sweater over a white shirt and tan cotton pants. His head was covered by a worn canvas hat with a narrow brim. He pressed a sketch pad firmly under his arm as he bent over to lock the grape-colored door, then turned and walked purposefully on the stepping stones and then westward on the narrow sidewalk toward Dennison Boulevard. Her imagination stayed with him as he boarded a dusty green bus and in a mile or so changed to another. She followed him as he walked on the tree-shaded sidewalks of Parkview Place and watched as he leaned on the Hartleys' fence and sketched the houses across the street. Then he was at St. Francis Park sitting on a bench, the sketch pad open on his lap, his hand drawing straight lines and curves as he watched two nannies push strollers down a pebbled path. And then?

Monica, sitting on her porch steps, waiting for Rob, shook her head impatiently. And then, *what?* She was jolted out of her thoughts by a voice close by.

"What'cha doing?" César had appeared from nowhere and was standing at the bottom of the steps looking up at her. He was not wearing the red baseball cap, and his thick mop of curly black hair hung loosely, seeming to diminish the size of his ears.

"Waiting for Rob," she said.

"Why?"

"You are nosy, aren't you?" She smiled at him. "But I'll tell you, anyway. We're going to look for El Pintor."

"Really? Do you know where he is?"

"Not exactly. But we'll find him." She jumped up. "Here's Rob. I'll see you later."

A dark blue pickup truck with Rob at the wheel made a broad U-turn on the street in front of her and came to a stop at the curb. Rob leaned across the seat and threw open the passenger-side door. "Sorry I'm late," he called. "Had to clean this limo. We spilled cola all over the back during the move yesterday, and that stuff dries sticky."

"You weren't that late," she said as she climbed onto the seat and buckled up.

"All set?" he asked.

She held up a large envelope. "All set," she answered. "I've got the drawings." They turned north on Dennison, and she said, "When you get to Evangeline, I can tell you how to go—if you want me to."

"I expect you to," he said.

She sat back and looked around. She'd never been in a truck before. The dashboard was different; there was very little on it. She wondered how he would know when the brake was on or the door left open. "Does this seat move?" she asked as she searched for a lever.

"I hope not," Rob said. "It's a bench seat. You're riding in a twelve-year-old Chevy."

After that she was quiet until she saw on her right a free-standing curbside marquee that said 'Talbot High Summer Session Begins on July 10.' Behind the marquee there was a short expanse of lawn and then a large, tired-looking two-story tan building. Five or six broad cement steps led to huge double doors. An almost empty parking lot was next to the building, while other smaller stucco buildings huddled around it.

"So this is Talbot High," Monica said.

Rob nodded. "My alma mater."

"My mother's, too. What's it like?"

Rob shrugged. "Just a school. You know, crowded classrooms and tired teachers who either don't know how to teach or are too busy handling the goof-offs to be able to teach."

"Sounds awful. But you must've learned something. You made it to college."

"U. C. Santa Barbara," Rob said with a grin. "All right, all right. I guess I made Talbot sound worse than it is. Maybe that's because I was one of the goof-offs when I first started there. I was a mess in middle school."

"What made you change?"

"There you go, jumping to conclusions again."

"Of course you changed," Monica said firmly.

Rob angled a quick look in her direction. "Yeah. I guess I did. It wasn't what, but who, helped me change, though. I owe a lot to El Pintor."

Monica stared at his profile thoughtfully. He's loyal, she thought. If anyone will find El Pintor, it's going to be Rob. "What else goes on at Talbot?" she said, deliberately changing the subject. "Extracurricular stuff, I mean. Clubs, sports, dances, you know."

"There are a few clubs, mostly for geeks and real computer nerds. And dances. Three or four a year."

"I love to dance. I'll bet you do, too."

"*Me? Dance?* Uh-uh. The closest I got to dancing was in my senior year after I'd gotten my letter in basketball. Three or four of us, wearing our letterman sweaters, of course, always showed up at the dances. We'd saunter in late, lean against the wall, and look disinterested. Hip, you know? Real cool."

Monica giggled softly. "I'll bet the girls loved that."

"Nobody loved it, except us." He grinned. "It took only one year away from it all to show me how stupid we were."

"Not stupid," Monica said. "Just kind of funny." She twisted in the seat, glancing over her shoulder for one last look at the school they had left behind. She wanted to ask, what kind of kids go there? But she knew better than to ask that of Rob. She wanted to ask, are there gangs? Do the kids smuggle in guns? Knives? How about dope? Are there a lot of kids at Talbot doing drugs? Yes, yes, yes. She was sure that yes was the answer to all of the above. So how could her father even consider letting her go to a school like that? But he was considering just that, and there was nothing to be done. She sighed.

"What's up?" Rob asked.

"Nothing. I was just thinking."

"We'll be at Evangeline in a couple of miles."

Once they had made the turn at Evangeline, it was only a matter of minutes until they were riding on streets so embracingly familiar that Monica's eyelids stung with tears. She knew every tree, every blade of green grass and every bloom on the apricot-colored bougainvillea growing over the Stanley's porte-cochere. She closed her eyes tightly and pressed her head against the vinyl-covered seat. Tears. This was not the time for tears. She kept her eyes closed, but her other senses were alive to the surroundings she knew so well. When she opened them again, the pickup truck was right where she had felt it would be: the corner of Parkview Place, with Mrs. Davenport's freshly painted white picket fence glimmering in the morning sun.

"Make a right here," she said. "And if you'll park by that first lamppost we can decide where to begin."

Rob turned and pulled over to the curb as she suggested. "I see your house," he said, indicating a two-story white house with dormer windows on the other side of the street. "That *is* your house, isn't it?"

"Not anymore," Monica said, and she had a hard time keeping the sadness she felt out of her voice. "My house is on Lucia. For a while, anyway."

"That's quite a come-down," Rob said, staring at the house.

Monica blushed. "It's different, that's all," she said and quickly pushed open the car door. "Should we start?"

"Sure. Where?"

"Up that way," she said. "At Jackie's house. The Bryles always get up early."

Rob glanced at his watch. "It's after ten. Is that early?"

"For some people it is." Monica started up the sidewalk. She had taken only a few steps when she heard Rob's voice raised in anger. "What's wrong?" she asked as she swung around.

The answer was immediate and clear. César, his black hair blown wildly, his face a picture of guilt and hope, was peering over the side of the bed of the pickup.

" . . . and if you think you're going to tag after us," Rob was saying, "you've got another thing coming. You're going to sit in the front of the truck and wait, even if we're gone for hours."

"But I came to look for El Pintor, too!" César wailed.

Rob turned to Monica. "You told him."

"I guess I did," she said. "I never dreamed he'd stow away."

"Well, he did."

"I can see that," she said stiffly. "I'm sorry."

The frown disappeared from Rob's face. "Anyway, it's not your fault. It's his." He yanked César out of the pickup. He planted him firmly on the ground and opened the door to the cab. "Go on, get in. And stay there. We'll be back in a while."

César stood quite still, his arms hanging limply at his sides. But his hands below his bony wrists were clenched tightly into fists. His black eyes seemed to darken as he looked up at Monica and said, "Please, Monica, I've been looking for El Pintor for a long time. Can't I come, too?"

Monica looked at Rob and then past him to the skinny little boy by the pickup's door. It means so much to him, she thought, but Rob is right. César, his T-shirt dotted with his breakfast cocoa, would not be an asset. She swallowed hard and said, "I don't think so, César. Do what Rob asks. We won't be too long."

"I hear you," the boy said sullenly, "but I don't like it." He got up on to the front seat and slammed the truck's door behind him.

Rob shrugged, and they started up the sidewalk together. "Here we are," Monica said, and they turned into the walkway of a large Spanish-style house. They pushed the button, and chimes sounded loudly. It was opened almost immediately.

"Monica!" the woman in the doorway said. "How nice of you to come and see us." She was a small, slim woman, deeply tanned, with short, flyaway blonde hair and clear blue eyes. She wore a short white tennis dress that revealed well-shaped athletic legs. "Come in, come in," she said. "But wouldn't you know it? We have a match at the club at eleven."

"That's okay, Mrs. Bryle," Monica said. "We can't stay either, so we won't come in. This is my friend Rob, and we just came to ask you a couple of questions."

Rob said how do you do and added, "We're looking for a friend of mine who's been gone for several days. We think that he spent some time on this block late last week."

"Here?" Mrs. Bryle said. "I don't remember any strange college boys—" She stopped. "Oh, dear, I don't mean strange, you know, I mean strangers."

"We know what you mean," Monica said, "but we're not looking for a college boy, anyway. Mr. Mead is . . ." She paused and looked at Rob . . . "close to seventy, I think." She drew out the sketches from the brown manila envelope that she held and handed Mrs. Bryle the one of Jana and Mr. Daniels. "Do you by any chance remember the man who drew this?"

"Why that's Jana," Mrs. Bryle said. "And I see why you think your Mr. Mead was here last week. This had to be done the day after school was out. That would be Thursday, wouldn't it? I know that for a fact because Jana and I had a row about her wearing that old faded T-shirt of Jackie's. Yes. And just after lunch, here came Mr. Daniels playing that horribly tinny 'Happy Days Are Here Again.' You remember, Monica. His truck is still clean and shiny, but that tune gets scratchier every year."

"So he was here!" Rob said eagerly. "Did you see where he went when he left?"

"I didn't see him at all," Mrs. Bryle said. "But he must have been here, else how could he have done that drawing?" She frowned as she studied the sketch. "From the angle he got of your house, Monica, I'd say he was standing in the Jeromes' front yard when he drew this."

"Of course," Monica said. "Leaning against the old elm."

"Well, *somebody* must've seen him," Rob said, a hint of impatience in his voice.

Monica glanced at him. She said "Jana" just as he said, "The little girl, of course," and they both turned to the woman at the door.

"Oh, my," she said. "Yes, Jana would be a help. Nothing gets by her. But she left this morning for a camping trip with my brother and his family. Heaven knows—or Jerry maybe—how you get in touch with people on the John Muir trail."

Monica stared at Mrs. Bryle, her feelings a mixture of disappointment and envy. Her father had promised her a wilderness experience, just for the two of them, and then his Washington, D.C., job had ruined it all. "Oh, that's too bad," she said and quickly added, "For us, I mean."

Mrs. Bryle said, "Maybe Mr. Daniels saw where your friend went. No, no, that wouldn't work. The ice-cream truck would have moved on." She sighed. "Yes, it's too bad about Jana. She probably talked to him. Even offered him some of her ice cream. You know Jana. She's much too friendly. We keep warning her . . ." Mrs. Bryle stopped abruptly, and a troubled frown grew on her face. She turned to Rob. "You say he's a friend of yours? And you know him, too, Monica?"

"Well, no," Monica said. "But my father does. And my mother did, too."

Mrs. Bryle nodded slowly, as if absorbing what they had just said. "Well, in that case," she said vaguely. And then,

"I'm sure someone else in the neighborhood saw him. Maybe one of the other neighbors can help you."

It was clear that they were dismissed. Monica said, "Please tell Jackie to call me when she returns." Rob said, "Thanks for your help, Mrs. Bryle." Then they walked to the sidewalk where they paused to decide which way to go.

"Rob," Monica said, "do you suppose she thought of something, something about that day that she didn't want to talk about?"

"Well, if she did, we'll never find out what it is by just standing here," Rob said impatiently. "Let's go knock on some more doors."

Chapter Nine

They did just that. Except for the friendly wel-
comes with which Monica was greeted, the visits
with her old neighbors were disappointing.

At the Ruzinskis' they sat in the kitchen, drank orange
juice, heard about a new grandchild, and learned nothing at
all about El Pintor. One good thing happened. Monica used
the kitchen phone to call Laurita and let her know how it
was that César was with them. And would she please let his
parents know?

Down the block, the Hodgkins family was leaving for a
weekend in the mountains, so Rob and Monica talked to
them standing by their car in the driveway. With no luck.
Monica watched the family drive off, as she waved goodbye
to their twin boys, neither of whom had remembered her.
That was when a realization plummeted from her heart to her
stomach. She was face-to-face with the fact that she was an
outsider in this place that for so long had been her home. She
was no longer a member of a circle of neighbors who had
been there for her since the day she was born. She closed her
eyes for a moment. There in her mind's eye was the street

called Lucia. She held back a grimace, cleared her throat, and turned to Rob. "Let's go see the Lloyds," she said.

Across the street the Lloyds were still in their robes. They apologized for not asking them in, but both Mr. and Mrs. Lloyd remained at the door to answer their questions. Mrs. Lloyd kept asking Monica questions about Washington, D.C., and about how her poor father was handling his sad situation. "It must be very hard for you," she said. Monica, acutely aware of Rob standing at her side, answered that they were doing fine. It was a struggle to stay on the subject of El Pintor. But they finally managed it and learned . . . nothing.

That was more or less the way it went on both sides of Parkview Place. No one had remembered seeing an old man with a sketch pad walking about their street on any day during the previous week, or any other day for that matter.

As they walked back to the pickup, Monica stole a quick glance at Rob. There was a frown on his face and a weary droop to his shoulders. He looked the way she felt. And why not? They had spent more than an hour knocking on doors and talking to people, and they had nothing to show for it. Besides, it was hot and humid. Above them the sun was intense in a sky the color of faded blue jeans, with wisps of white cloud scattered here and there.

They walked silently for a few moments, and then she spoke. "I guess we got a bunch of nothing, didn't we?"

"Yeah."

"Maybe that's all we'll get at St. Francis Park, but we ought to go there, too, don't you think?"

"Yeah. I guess so."

She glanced at Rob again, ready to say, you don't have to be so sour with me, but the sight of Rob's face stopped her. He looked sad, miserably sad. Quickly, she turned away. Her feelings had changed from annoyance to something soft and warm she had no name for, but that made her heart beat faster. Then, wanting to make him feel better, she said, "A lot of nannies take kids there nearly every day. Maybe one of them saw him there."

Rob ran his hand through his hair in exasperation. "It's Saturday," he said. "They don't work on Saturdays."

"Some of them do," Monica said. "So let's go. It's only a few blocks away, but maybe we ought to drive there because I don't think we should leave César—" She stopped in mid-sentence and in mid-stride. "Look at that! What's happening?"

César, his black locks flying, hurtled down the center of the street toward them. Chasing some yards behind him was a heavyset man who shouted angrily, "You little hoodlum, stop! I told you to stop!"

César, now close to Rob and Monica, stopped, turned, and yelled, "It's them! I told you! See? Here they are!" He angled toward the sidewalk, jumped over the curb, and grabbed Monica's hand.

The stocky man slowed down to a walk as he got on the sidewalk and went forward to meet them. He wore dark blue pants and a light blue short-sleeved shirt that had the words Walsh Security and the name Henry, on its pocket. His breathing was shallow and rapid as he reached them, but that didn't stop him from talking. "Are you two responsible for this nosy kid?" he said, panting. "You're not his parents, are you?"

Monica's face grew red. "Of course we're not," she said crossly. "He's eight and I'm almost seventeen. You figure it out." César's hot little hand was still in hers, and she swung him around to face her. "Is that what you told him?"

"No way," César grumbled. "I didn't tell him nothing. Just that I came here with you guys."

"Yeah," Rob said, "and uninvited." He turned to the older man. "But he's with us, all right."

The security man ignored Rob's statement. Instead, he said, "That truck down the way belong to you?"

Rob's shoulders tightened. "The blue one? Yes, it's mine. And César had my permission to sit in it."

"Did he have your permission to go snooping in people's yards and through their windows, too?"

"Dammit, César!" Rob said. "I told you to stay in the truck."

"He don't mind very well," the security man said. "He was across the street, scaring the stuffing out of Mrs. Berger and her father. According to Mrs. Berger, he kept pounding on her den window and shouting names at them."

César looked sheepish. "I thought he was El Pintor. For a minute, anyway. I was gonna go back to the truck, honest, but this guy grabbed me." César smiled, a wide smile that showed most of his remarkably white teeth. "But I got away. When he wouldn't listen to me, I got loose of him. And here we are." He looked up proudly at Monica.

Yes, here we are, Monica thought, but *where?* The security man's really annoyed at César—at all of us, maybe— and Rob's getting exasperated. He's running his hand through his hair again. I guess we'd better apologize for César, and maybe he won't bother us anymore.

The security man mopped his face on a crumpled white handkerchief. He frowned at them as he said, "You three sure don't belong in this neighborhood. So what're you doing here?"

Monica stiffened and drew in her breath, but before she could say anything, Rob said, "We're exactly where we belong. And we're doing exactly what we came for. Where do you get off butting into our business?"

The older man looked as if he were about to explode. "This smart aleck here," he sputtered, "sure wasn't where he belonged. He—"

"Yes, he was!" Monica interrupted. "He thought he'd found our friend. I'll bet Mrs. Berger's father looked just like El Pintor."

"Yeah, he did," César said. "Kinda."

"Besides, Mrs. Berger's deaf as a rock," Monica added. "So how would she know he was shouting?"

"And how would you know she was deaf?" the security man asked.

"Because I lived next door to her for years," Monica answered. "This is my old neighborhood." *My old neighborhood.* The words had a dull, dead sound. She sighed, then quickly told herself that this was not the time to mope. If she was going to mope, there was plenty of time for that later. "Look, Mr. . . . Mr. Henry," she said, "maybe you know something about our friend. He was around here last week doing some drawings, and then he just disappeared, like into thin air. And we're trying to find him." Rob was giving her a disapproving look. His face was flushed, his eyes fiery. He doesn't want me to ask anything of this man, she thought. He'd rather punch him in the nose.

The man named Henry looked at Monica for a long moment, then said, "This friend of yours, what kind of a man is he?" He was speaking now in a smooth, quiet voice.

Monica looked at Rob. Rob shook his head, so she turned back to the man before her and said, "Why, he's a very good man, of course."

"No, no, no, that's not what I mean. What does he look like? And is he . . . is he . . . What I mean is, does he hit on all cylinders?"

Now Rob spoke. "El Pin—Mr. Mead's not crazy, criminal, or a drug user, if that's what you mean," he said angrily. "Unless it's crazy to wear a white painter's cap, because he wears one everywhere he goes. He's okay. He's healthy and he's intelligent."

Monica gave her head a little shake. There went her picture of El Pintor in his gray sweater and brimmed canvas hat. It occurred to her that she had no idea at all what he really looked like. And it also occurred to her that she very much wanted to know.

"Well," the man named Henry said, scratching his head. "The painter's hat does it. I just might know where your friend is."

Monica drew in her breath as Rob said, "You might? Where? Where is he?"

"Monica!" César said, tugging at her arm. "He's found him!"

"I wouldn't jump for joy just yet," Henry said. "The news isn't all that good. The man I'm thinking might be your friend is in bad shape. He don't even know who he is or where he belongs. Not even what year this is."

"That's not El Pintor," César mumbled.

"It might be," Henry said. "This fellow—whatever his name is, El Something or Mead—took quite a bump on the head. The doctors at Westside Emergency called it a concussion."

"Where is he?" Rob asked. "At the hospital?"

"No. He's just a couple of blocks away. With a family called Callahan."

"The Callahans?" Monica said. "I can't believe it." She turned to Rob. "Are they friends of his?"

Rob shook his head. "I don't know. I don't think so."

"What's he doing at the Callahans'?" Monica asked.

"It's a long story," Henry said. "Why don't we just go see Mrs. Callahan and find out what's what, before you hear the whole thing."

"You go, Rob," Monica said, suddenly feeling awkward. If it was El Pintor, he wouldn't need a stranger barging in on him. "I'll stay with César."

"Why?" Henry asked. "Don't you know the Callahans?"

"A little," Monica said. "I was in the same Girl Scout troop as their daughter Katy."

"Well, then, you oughtta come. The kid can wait outside."

"No," Monica said firmly. "If I go, then César goes, too. After all, El Pintor might recognize him."

Henry shook his head and shrugged. He pulled a cellular phone from his shirt pocket and punched the buttons. "I'll let the Callahans know we're coming," he said.

They followed Henry's car to a house on a corner two blocks west of Parkview Place. Monica remembered the high brick wall that bordered the street side of the low rambling house. She remembered, too, throwing Katy's rolled-up sleeping bag over those bricks on their return from a Girl Scout outing and the heart-stopping sound of breaking branches as the bag landed in Mrs. Callahan's treasured rose garden. She shook that memory away as Rob parked at the curb by the fence. They left the pickup and walked to the front of the house, leaving behind the sound of children's squeals and laughter on the other side of the wall.

Henry waited for them at the front door. Before he could ring the bell, the door was thrown open, and the small dark-haired woman who opened it said breathlessly, "Oh, I'm so glad you're here. I do hope you can tell us who our Mr. Good Man is."

She waved them into a wood-paneled entry hall that led on one side to a large, airy sitting room; on the other, to a room with a large dining table that was set for a meal with grass mats and colorful ceramic dishes. A delicious aroma of garlic and spices and tomato sauce filled the entry hall.

"We're keeping you from your lunch," Monica said, her mouth watering.

Mrs. Callahan shook her head. "It doesn't matter. That's just a topping for pizza. It'll wait. This is too important." She led them down a long hall with doors on each side. Two or three were open, showing bedrooms in different stages of disarray. Clothes and toys were strewn on the rugs, and on the furniture, and in one particularly scattered room, a boy of about twelve was eagerly pushing buttons on the keyboard of a computer. The hall ended in a glass-enclosed den with French doors that opened to the rear garden. Mrs. Callahan said, "Come this way. He's outside with the children."

The open doorway framed a garden scene that was as tranquil as a lullaby. It's like a painting, Monica thought, a painting of what my art teacher called "Americana." The children were two little blonde girls of about eight and six. They both wore rumpled khaki shorts and striped T-shirts, and were kicking a beach ball over the grass toward a bench on which sat an elderly man wearing a white painter's cap. As she watched, the man on the bench removed his cap and gingerly rubbed his head along the sides of a bandage above his right temple. He had thick white hair that was brushed over the tops of his ears and a face that was thin and angular. Even sitting, it was clear that he was quite tall and that his body, too, was spare.

Mrs. Callahan pushed open the screen door, but only César went through. He flew down the shallow steps and across the grass, calling, "It's El Pintor! It's El Pintor!"

The man on the bench looked up. "Hello, young man," he said with a smile. "Did you come to play with Peg and Annie?"

César stopped, threw a glance over his shoulder at the people in the house, then turned back to the man on the bench. "Mr. Mead," he said loudly, "Mr. Mead, it's me, César!"

The man returned the white cap to his head, a puzzled frown on his face. "César," he said slowly and frowned more deeply.

César's face had grown red. "Come on," he said plaintively, "you know me. I know you do!"

The two girls ran to the man's side. "Go away!" the older girl said. "Leave him alone!"

"Leave Mr. Good Man alone!" the little one cried. "He's my friend."

In the house Monica asked, "Rob, is that El Pintor?" When he nodded, she said, "But he doesn't seem to know César."

"Amnesia," Mrs. Callahan said. "Dr. Hilger hopes it will be temporary. I hoped he'd snap out of it when he saw someone he knew."

"Go talk to him, Rob," Monica said urgently. "He'll know you, won't he?"

"I think so. I hope so." Rob straightened his shoulders and went outside. "Mr. Mead," he called as he crossed to the bench, "it's Rob. We've been looking for you."

El Pintor shook his head. "Have you?" he said. "I'm sorry. It's just that I can't remember . . . I can't remember . . . something." He smiled a weak, embarrassed smile. "But it will come back to me soon. Now, who are you and what were you saying?"

"Margaret! Elizabeth Anne!" Mrs. Callahan called. "Come in the house for a minute."

The older girl said, "Come on, Annie," and took her little sister's hand. They walked toward the house, but every step they took was slow and heavy with reluctance. At the door, they brushed by Monica and their mother and raced down the long hall, yelling for their brother.

Outside in the garden, Rob was seated on the bench by El Pintor, with César squatting on the lawn a few feet away. Rob was saying, "I'm Roberto, Mr. Mead, Roberto Almayo, remember? We painted the outside of your studio last summer. Remember the purple door?"

El Pintor shrugged and shook his head. "I want to remember," he said heavily. "I want to remember, but I can't. Look, young man, are you sure you know who I am? Do I really have a studio? What do I do there? And what's this about a purple door?"

Monica, standing at the open door, swallowed hard, fighting to keep tears back. She could hear the desperate longing in the old man's voice. He wanted a clue, a thread, no matter how fragile, to connect him to his past. She pushed open the screen doors and went down the steps. "Rob," she called, "tell him about Sopa. Maybe if—" But that was all she said.

El Pintor was on his feet, hurrying toward her. "Cristina," he called. "Cristina, it's you! My girl, how I've missed you."

Chapter Ten

Monica's first thought was that she should correct him. "No, no, I'm not Cristina," she started to say, but immediately changed her mind. El Pintor needed something, or someone, to cling to, and, besides, he was standing before her, his hands outstretched, waiting for hers. Hurriedly, she put her hands in his and returned his smile.

Behind her Mrs. Callahan said, "Thank God, he does know you." To El Pintor she said, "So Cristina's a friend of yours. That's wonderful. You'll be remembering everything now." There was a smile dancing through her words.

"Yes," El Pintor said, "yes." He searched Monica's face. "I did remember you, didn't I?"

Monica threw a troubled glance first at Rob and then at Mrs. Callahan. "Yes," she said. "Yes, you did."

Rob, who was standing behind El Pintor, shook his head slowly. A puzzled frown appeared on Mrs. Callahan's face at Rob's gesture, and he said quickly, "Could we talk somewhere?"

Mrs. Callahan nodded. "Mr. Good Man," she said, "Peg and Annie are waiting to have lunch with you, and I have to talk with this young man. Let's just go to the dining room and get you started. The little boy, too. Come on," she called to César. "There's plenty for all."

"Cristina," El Pintor said, holding her hand tightly, "you'll come, too, won't you?"

With a glance at Rob, who signaled go ahead, Monica said, "Sure. If it's all right with Mrs. Callahan."

There was only one empty place left at the dining room table when finally all were seated. Mrs. Callahan and her twelve-year-old son, Mike, brought out two huge pizzas, placed them on the table, and filled all their glasses with milk. Then she brought in a bowl of fruit salad and a stack of small dishes and excused herself.

Monica stared at the empty doorway, wishing she could go with her. There was so much she wanted to know. Especially—she glanced around the table at all the Callahan faces—how did El Pintor come to be here? And stumbling on that thought came another. What was *she* doing here? Oh, she'd sat at this table before dressed in a Girl Scout uniform, but on that day she had belonged. Today she was no longer Monica from Parkview; today she was Monica from a *barrio* that still felt foreign to her. And to add to her feelings of confusion, she wasn't even Monica; for the moment she was Cristina. Her jumble of thoughts was interrupted by a shout from Mike.

"Stop it, Peg!" he yelled as she reached for the pizza. "Mom said, 'company first'! Mr. Good Man," he added, "you and your friends go first." Mike, a somber-faced red-head with deep-set brown eyes, was obviously going to run the show at the table. Once El Pintor's, Monica's, and César's plates were filled, he helped his sisters to their pizza. "The one with lots of pepperoni," Peg ordered, and Annie had to have "the piece without green gunk on it."

After that there was an awkward silence until Annie said, "How come you know them, Mr. Good Man? Where'd they come from?"

El Pintor, who had removed his cap upon entering the house, ran his hand through his hair and shook his head. "I don't know, Annie," he said quietly. "I just don't know."

Annie gave him a wondering look. "But you called her Cristina," she said. "How come?"

César quickly swallowed a mouthful of pizza and said, "That isn't even her—"

"César!" Monica interrupted. She leaned across the table and said to Annie, "That's what he calls me. Don't I look as if my name's Cristina?"

"I guess," Annie said sullenly, and they were quiet once more.

It was El Pintor who broke this silence. "Cristina," he said, "are you going to take me to where I live?"

Monica, surprised by the question, was struck dumb for a moment. Rob, she thought, come back. I need you. She was about to say yes when César spoke.

"Not just her, Mr. Mead," he said emphatically. "We're all gonna take you. In Rob's truck."

El Pintor looked at Monica. "Mead," he said. "Is that my name?"

Monica nodded. "All your paintings say Francis Mead." Immediately she was sorry she had mentioned his paintings. She'd opened up a new box of questions. And, actually, what did she know about that?

El Pintor, however, was dwelling on something else. "I wish I could remember," he said. "They tell me I got a bump on the head—"

"Saving me!" Annie shouted. "I told you already. Mommy says you're a hero."

"Sure, he's a hero," Mike said seriously. "And, Mr. Good Man, you don't have to go. Dad says you can stay here as long as you want."

Monica stopped eating. Hero? How? When? But before she could ask anything, two things happened in quick succession. Mrs. Callahan appeared in the doorway and asked El Pintor to go back to the den with her. And no sooner had they left than the front door opened and closed, and another brown-eyed redhead walked into the room.

"Any pizza left for me?" Katy Callahan said. Monica turned and looked at Katy with surprise. Gone were the pimples and the shaggy ponytail. This girl had peaches-and-cream skin and shiny auburn hair that hung straight and loose below her chin line. "Well, don't all answer at once," Katy said when she got no response. And then, "Oh, good, there's plenty." She slid into the empty chair.

As she did, Annie said, "That's Cristina over there. She's Mr. Good Man's friend." Then, pointing to César, "He is, too. But his name's funny."

"Where *is* Mr. Good Man?" Katy asked, her eyes moving to the empty chair by Monica. Then she looked at Monica. "Hey, don't I know you?"

"You should," Monica said. "We were in Girl Scouts together."

Katy paused, a wedge of pizza almost to her mouth. "Hey, we were, weren't we? But there's something that's bothering me."

"It's the 'Cristina,'" Monica said with a smile. "My name's Monica Ramos. El Pin—Mr. Good Man thinks I'm my mother Cristina, so . . ." She shrugged. "So we haven't told him I'm not."

"Monica!" Katy shrilled. "Monica Ramos! Why aren't you in Washington?"

"Because my . . . because it didn't . . ." She stopped fumbling and said, "It's a long story. We just don't live there anymore."

"She lives on my street," César piped up. "A street called Lucia. So does El Pintor."

"Lucia?" Katy said between bites of pizza. "I know where that is. We got my guitar on the corner of Lucia and Dennison. It's absolutely elegant. My guitar, that is. Wait'll I finish eating, Monica, and I'll show it to you."

At that moment Mrs. Callahan came into the room. "Hullo, Katy," she said and then addressed herself to Monica. "Mr. Good . . ." She stopped and shook her head. "It's so difficult changing names. Anyway, Mr. Mead's ready to go home now. That is, if Cristina's going with him." She caught the look on Katy's face and said, "I know, I know, but I need to call her Cristina for a while."

Monica pushed her chair back and got up.

Mrs. Callahan went on talking. "I've packed his belongings in a small bag. When we brought him here, all he had was what he was wearing, so we bought him a few things." Mrs. Callahan smiled. "Including a white painter's cap. He didn't want to leave the hospital without his, and his wasn't wearable. And glasses. He definitely needs glasses for close up. We got him a pair of drugstore glasses." She looked around the table. "I called your father, kids. He says to tell you that we'll go visit Mr. Good Man soon. But right now why don't you all go say goodbye to him."

There was a general scraping of chairs and a rush of footsteps as the four young Callahans left the dining room. César jumped up, too.

"I'll go be with El Pintor," he said. "He might need me."

The two women watched César leave and then Mrs. Callahan said, "I guess the young man, Rob, told me all I need to know about Mr. . . . Mr. Mead. Such as where he lives and what he does. Not just that he paints, but other things he's done. We called him right when we called him Mr. Good Man, didn't we?"

Monica nodded. She knew that Annie and Mike had called him a hero. She knew that Rob's mother thought he was a saint. And she knew that he was her mother's best friend. But that was all she knew. She wanted to know more.

Mrs. Callahan nodded, too, and said, "Up to now, you're the only one he remembers from his past."

"Not me. He remembers Cristina."

"But it's a start."

"I know," Monica said, but what she was thinking was, what will happen when he finds out I'm not?

"I'm going into the kitchen to have a bite to eat with Rob," Mrs. Callahan said, "and then we'll go." At the look on Monica's face she added, "Oh, yes, I'm going to drive you there. You and Mr. Good Man. There's not much room in Rob's truck, is there?"

When Mrs. Callahan left, Monica stood at the dining room window, looking outside. A light breeze ruffled the sun-glistened leaves of the trees lining the street. A woman and a very small boy in red-and-blue overalls walked slowly under the trees, the boy stopping every now and then to pick up some fallen leaves. Everything looked ordinary and peaceful out there. She frowned. There was nothing ordinary and peaceful about her mood. She felt trapped and she didn't like it. It had all happened so fast. And innocently. She was in this muddle because she had wanted to help Rob find El Pintor. No, that wasn't exactly fair. She, too, had wanted to find El Pintor. And because of that, here she was, pretending to be someone she wasn't. Why had Cristina— someone from the distant past—sparked something in El

Pintor's mind that Rob and César hadn't? And why had she gone along with it? Pretending to be Cristina might turn out to be very unfair to a nice old man. Unfair and maybe even harmful. At the sound of footsteps she swung around.

"Monica," Rob said, entering the room. "We're going on ahead. I called Toni. She's going down to straighten up the studio." He grinned. "Anyway, I think that's what she said. She was so excited, she didn't make much sense."

"That's good," she said dully. "Look, Rob, nobody's told me anything about El Pintor. All I know is what the kids said about his being a hero. He really must be. They've practically made him one of the family."

"I know."

"I know you know," she said sharply, "but you're not the only one. I want to know, too."

Rob looked at her in surprise. "Hey, what did I do?"

"You didn't do anything. It's just that . . ." She stopped. Could she really explain? Could she say, everyone else is running everything, making decisions for me, and I'm the one caught in the middle.

"I'll tell you all I know when we're back home," he said. "While we were in the den, Mrs. Callahan called the doctor, and they're both hoping that there'll be another face on Lucia that will trigger his memory."

"I guess we're all hoping that," Monica said.

"Right." Rob poked his head into the hallway. "César," he called, "come on!"

Twenty minutes later, with a full contingent of Calla-hans standing at the curb waving goodbye, Mrs. Callahan, Monica, and El Pintor also started off for Lucia Street.

"Don't hesitate to back-seat drive," Mrs. Callahan told Monica, who was with her in the front seat of her van. "I have a general idea of where I'm going and that's all."

Monica said, "Thanks, I will," and then they all fell silent. Except for a couple of questions from Mrs. Callahan to El Pintor, asking him if anything was familiar, the entire conversation during the ride was limited to instructions from Monica regarding stops, turns, and streets.

Beginning at the point where they passed Talbot High, Monica felt herself becoming extremely uncomfortable. The neighborhood was getting seedier. Although she had become somewhat used to the shabbiness that existed on this part of Dennison Boulevard, she was seeing it today through Mrs. Callahan's eyes. It embarrassed her, as if the occasional graf-fiti and garish signs were her doing. When they turned onto Lucia, she felt a little shudder, and when the Callahan's van neared her house, the sight of the faded paint and loose-hanging shutter made her want to hide. She took a deep breath and said, "There. That's it. The house with the long, narrow building filling its driveway."

Rob's blue truck was parked at the curb by the studio. Standing on the sidewalk beyond it was a small crowd of people. Rob and Toni were in the forefront. They waved, smiling broadly. Three boys surrounded César, who was talking and pointing at the Callahans' van. Behind the boys were two older women who were solemn-faced and silent. And coming up the passageway between the studio and the house was Laurita and Laurita's nephew from the guitar shop.

A sudden hush fell on everyone as the van pulled up to the curb and Rob hurried forward to push open the door for El Pintor and Monica. Mrs. Callahan came around the front of her car carrying two small bags that held El Pintor's belongings.

El Pintor smiled at Rob, then looked around at all the expectant faces. He threw a bewildered look at Monica.

"That's your studio," she said hurriedly. "See the purple door?"

He nodded. "Yes, I see. Cristina, are all these people my friends?"

Chapter Eleven

Inside his living room, El Pintor looked around with sharp interest, but, except for a troubled frown or two, there was no sign of recognition. "This is where I live?" It was a question directed at Monica.

She nodded, and Mrs. Callahan quickly said, "It's a nice room. Warm. Livable. I especially like the rugs."

El Pintor stood for several minutes looking at the books that filled the hanging shelves on the west wall. He pulled out a copy of *Moby Dick* and leafed through it. The soft rustle of the pages was the only sound in the room, and the remaining silence was as pressing as a prayer. Abruptly, with a quick shake of his head, El Pintor returned the book to its shelf and walked to the corner of the room with the small sink and stove. He opened the refrigerator door. Its shallow shelves were crowded with bowls of salad and fruit and cartons of milk and juice. He closed it and glanced at a casserole on the counter. "Someone's been cooking," he said gently.

Behind him, Toni swallowed hard and nodded. "My aunt sent you those enchiladas. She knows how much you like them."

"Thank her for me," he said, without looking around. And then, with a long, drawn-out sigh, he turned. He looked extremely weary as he glanced from Toni, to Rob, to Monica, and then to Mrs. Callahan. "I don't remember anything," he said in a low voice.

"That's all right," Mrs. Callahan said. "Don't try so hard. Dr. Hilger said it will just happen." She snapped her fingers as she said the last words.

Toni, fighting back tears, cleared her throat and said, "The studio's this way." She opened the door at the back of the small room, and Monica went on ahead of El Pintor. She wanted to see his face when he looked at the paintings that lined the walls.

Nothing. El Pintor walked around the studio, carefully examining the sketches and tools on the worktable, and, with even more deliberation, he studied the paintings on the walls and those stacked on the floor. The other four watched him eagerly. El Pintor turned to them and said, "So I did these? I don't remember." Their disappointment was palpable, filling the room like a thick fog.

Shortly after, Mrs. Callahan left, assuring El Pintor that she and the children would be back to see him in a day or two. Toni, Rob, and Monica left, too, but not before they wrote down their telephone numbers and not before Monica pointed out her bedroom window, which was almost directly across from the small window above El Pintor's kitchen sink. He had nodded and smiled and said, "Of course. That's how we send special messages, isn't it?"

Later, as she waited on the front porch for Rob to return, Monica wondered if those words of El Pintor's contained a memory or merely a suggestion. It was strange that only Cristina triggered his memory. You would have thought he'd remember Rob and César more easily. Well, there was no sense in trying to figure it out. She tapped her toe impatiently. Where was Rob? He'd called, "I'll be back to tell you everything," when Toni and he had started for home. And that was more than twenty minutes ago.

She fought back her irritation. Rob's family, people who had known El Pintor for many, many years, deserved to hear the story of his disappearance before she did. After all, she had only met El Pintor today. Still, she *was* the one who had found him.

A screen door slammed at the far end of the street, and Monica turned in time to see Licha, César's sister, step out of their house. Josie, Licha's redheaded friend, was sitting under their tree in the hanging tire. She rose slowly and said something to Licha, and then the two girls moved leisurely down the block. When they were directly across the street from Monica, they stopped. Josie whispered something to Licha, and they broke out into loud laughter. In a couple of minutes, they stopped laughing and angled across the street to the torn-down car and the boys working on it.

Monica leaned forward to look for Rob. She could see only a small section of the rear of the car because the front of the studio hid the rest, but she could hear the clinks and clangs of tools on metal and the hum, if not the words, of the boys' conversation. As Licha and Josie crossed the street, there was a sudden burst of sound from the car's engine and yells of elation from the boys. Almost as suddenly, the engine died and the voices rose in argument.

Josie called, "Hi, what's up?" and got no answer. "Hey, I said . . ." she started, but another look at the boys standing by the car kept her from going on. She and Licha stopped at the edge of the sidewalk, the green stripe in Josie's dyed red hair gleaming in the mid-afternoon sun. They were clearly annoyed. When they saw Rob approaching, they ran up to him, flanking him on either side. Rob, too, it seemed, disappointed them. Whatever question it was that they asked, he gave a quick answer to and left them standing open-mouthed and chagrined once more. He gave a brief nod of greeting to the grumbling mechanics and lengthened his stride as he hurried toward Monica.

"I know, I know," he said as he sat down beside her. "It's about time."

Monica shrugged. "I didn't say it."

"Yeah," Rob answered with a grin, "but you looked it. You probably guessed what kept me. They had to know everything at my house. They're old friends of his, you know."

Instead of answering, Monica looked over her shoulder into the house and called, "Laurita! Rob's here. Should we—"

"I'm right here," Laurita said from the other side of the screen door. "I'll come out there with you."

They moved up onto the porch then. Monica and Laurita sat in the two porch chairs and Rob leaned against the railing facing them.

"It's not a long story," he said. "And it's typical of El Pintor. I remember once when I was a little kid, he climbed that tree in César's yard to bring down a kitten that had been chased up there by two of the neighborhood's meanest dogs. He didn't even—"

"Rob!" Monica interrupted. "You're doing it on purpose."

"If you don't tell us what happened," Laurita said with an impish grin that belied her age, "we're going to beat up on you." Monica glanced at her and thought, no wonder my mother liked her.

"What happened," Rob said, "was that he saved little Annie's life." He paused, his black eyes sparkling with mischief.

"Don't stall," Monica said. "Now we want the details. All of them. And no more goofing off."

"I hear you, I hear you," Rob said and, with no more hesitation, plunged somberly into the story.

Mrs. Callahan, he said, and the two little girls had been at St. Francis Park on that Thursday afternoon. Annie and Peggy were kicking a soccer ball around while their mother sat on a bench watching them. The two girls were arguing about who could kick the ball farther. Finally, Peggy gave the ball a kick that sent it flying over Annie's head. With a shriek of glee, Peggy plopped down on the grass and said "You've gotta go get it," to Annie. Annie, grumbling, trudged after the ball past some shrubs that hid her from view.

After a minute, Peggy called, "Hey, slowpoke, hurry up!" When there was no answer, Mrs. Callahan hurried past the shrubbery to look for her. She was just in time to see Annie at the edge of the street, holding the ball and talking to a man who leaned out of the open passenger door of an ancient gray sedan. As Mrs. Callahan called to Annie, the man bent down and grabbed Annie's arm, sending the ball flying and dragging her halfway into the car.

Mrs. Callahan screamed, "Stop! Stop!"

Annie yelled, "Mama-a-a-a!"

Out of nowhere, El Pintor appeared, executing the fastest, longest, and, according to Mrs. Callahan, the most magnificent flying football tackle she had ever seen. He grasped Annie's legs and pulled her away from the stranger's hold. Almost immediately, the gray sedan shot forward, and the open door swung back, striking El Pintor on the head and sending both of them rolling to the ground beside the curb. With its open door swinging, the gray car screeched up the street in a cloud of smoking rubber. When Mrs. Callahan reached the curb, she found Annie scratched and screaming, lying face down at El Pintor's feet.

The little girl reached up to her mother, but El Pintor, who was lying on his back, one hand dangling over the curb, didn't move. It was clear that he was unconscious. There was an ugly open gash on his forehead near his temple that was bleeding profusely. Mrs. Callahan immediately called the paramedics on her cellphone and, while they waited for them, stripped Annie of her T-shirt to stem the bleeding on El Pintor's head.

A neighbor was called who came for the girls, and Mrs. Callahan followed the ambulance to the emergency room. There, El Pintor regained consciousness, but didn't know who he was, what day it was, or what city he was in. There was absolutely nothing on him to identify him. The only clue was a bus transfer, so, although they searched the park for any of his belongings, they gave up the idea of looking for a car that might have been his.

The diagnosis was that he had a mild concussion and that he would be fine with a few days' rest. As for the amnesia? That, too, Mrs. Callahan was assured, would disappear in a day or two. By that time Mr. Callahan had arrived at the hospital, and he arranged to have El Pintor released to them.

The following day, they took him to see Dr. Hilger, a neurologist, who agreed with the diagnosis. When several days went by and there was no break in the amnesia, Mr. Callahan had started to make inquiries in the neighborhood of St. Francis Park, but he had gotten nowhere.

"We know how frustrated he must have been, don't we?" Rob ended. "And how glad he must have been when we showed up."

"Right," Monica said. "What a story. No wonder they call him Mr. Good Man."

Laurita nodded and sighed. "He is a good man," she said. "We must do everything we can to help him."

Chapter Twelve

Rob let out a deep breath and sat back wearily in the porch chair. Monica shook her head. Rob had filled in some empty places in the story, but it wasn't complete yet. It was good to sit quietly. The peaceful moment didn't last. Loud voices reached her from the studio. Monica jumped up. "Hey, what's going on over there?" she called.

Rob rushed down the steps with Laurita and Monica close behind. Licha sat on the edge of one of the turquoise benches by El Pintor's door, looking as if she was ready to run. Josie stood at the open door facing El Pintor. He ran his fingers through his thick white hair and shook his head slowly as he listened to Josie.

"Come on, old man," she was saying, "of course you remember me. Don't give me that gaff. Just pay up the forty bucks you owe me."

"Hey, Josie!" Rob shouted. "What's all that about?"

"None of your business," Josie grumbled. "It's between him and me."

Licha popped off the bench and raced through the flowers to meet Rob. "It wasn't my idea," she said breathlessly. "I told her it wouldn't work."

"What wouldn't work?"

Licha looked down at her toes. They were painted black and extended from a pair of garish red sandals. Monica, on the sidewalk with Laurita and only a yard away from Licha, had trouble hearing her as she replied in a voice that was barely above a whisper. "We—well, Josie figured if he couldn't remember anything, he'd have to give her money if she told him he owed it to her."

"Shut up!" Josie bellowed over her shoulder. "Don't be such a chicken!"

Rob scowled as he swung around toward Josie. "I've heard of scams," he growled, "but this is the lowest. Josie! Get away from that door now, this minute, immediately, or else I'll move you myself."

"Nobody tells me what to do," Rosie yelled, throwing Rob an angry look.

Rob took a step toward the door and said, "Did you hear me, Josie? Go! Now!"

Josie took another look at him and, ignoring the flowers, trampled through them at a distance from Rob and then raced across the street. Licha elbowed by Monica and Laurita and flew after her.

At the door, El Pintor stood shaking his head, and then he caught sight of Monica. "Cristina," he called, "those aren't your friends, are they?"

Monica shook her head, and Laurita looked at her with a puzzled frown. "No," Monica called to El Pintor and quickly whispered to Laurita, "He thinks I'm Cristina. I forgot to tell you."

El Pintor stepped outside. "Well, that's good," he said. "They're not right for you, Cristina. So where's that little best friend of yours? What was she called? Lorie? Lorraine?"

Monica didn't know what to say. She looked from Laurita to Rob and back again. It was Laurita who answered.

"She's been gone for a while, Señor Mead," she said, "but she'll be back soon, I hope."

Monica looked at her with gratitude and thought, I can't keep this up too long. It's a silly game, anyway. And what good does it do? He needs to live now, not in the past.

"I hope so, too," El Pintor said and turned to Rob. "Thank you for sending off those girls. They took me by surprise. I'll be able to handle pranksters on my own from now on."

Rob's grin stretched from one side of his face to the other. "You sound just like your old self," he said.

El Pintor returned the grin. "I *am* my old self, with some of the machinery malfunctioning."

"Not for long," Rob said.

Please not for long, Monica thought.

Laurita said "*Dios quiera,*" and quickly translated, "God willing." Then she added, "Señor Mead, why don't you come have supper with Moni—with us. We won't be eating for a couple of hours yet, so you'll have plenty of time to rest."

"Thank you, no," El Pintor replied. "That's very kind of you, but I'd better spend some time in these rooms where people tell me I've lived for so many years. Maybe some of the paintings or papers, or the feel of the bed, will awaken my memory. As for food, I won't starve, will I? My little kitchen is bulging with everyone's gifts." He looked at Laurita. "Maybe, miss, you would suggest how I should heat the enchiladas?"

"I'll be glad to," Laurita said, starting up the stepping stones that led to his door. "And, Señor Mead, you may have forgotten, but I'm called Laurita."

El Pintor gave her a troubled look, shook his head as if to clear it, and held open his door for her to enter.

"It's so sad," Monica said as Rob and she returned to the porch and settled in the chairs. "Will he ever remember?"

"Sure, he will. Give him time. It's been a funny day for all of us. Half good and half bad and, for some dumb reason, pretty tiring. And it's still not over for me. I promised Al—he's my cousin—to help him move his refrigerator tonight."

"Why?" Monica said. "Why you? Why doesn't he hire a mover?"

"Because," Rob said, angling a wry glance at her, "because my price is right."

"Oh. Did he ask for bids?"

"No, Monica. He asked for help. He doesn't have the money for a mover. And even if he did, he's got a cousin with a truck and a reasonable amount of strength, so why look anywhere else?"

Monica stiffened. "Look, Rob," she said, "maybe I'm stupid, but I thought I'd only asked a question. Didn't I just get a sermon about something?"

"Yeah," Rob said, his face reddening. "Not exactly a sermon, though. More like a lesson on how people manage when they're broke. But I guess it's not up to me to teach you."

"No, it isn't. Even if I do have a lot to learn."

Rob leaned forward in the chair, his elbow on his knee, his chin in his hand. After a moment he sat back. "I'm always putting my foot in my mouth with you. Sorry."

Monica smiled. "I'm kind of sorry, too, so let's forget it. Anyway, where were we?"

"I was just saying that I wish I didn't have to help haul that refrigerator." He shot a look at her, then studied his hands as he said, "Maybe then you and I could take in a movie or something."

"I'd like that," she said softly, and then she had to clear her throat, and that sounded so loud it embarrassed her.

"Good," he said and drew in his breath as if he had been holding it. "Let's make it tomorrow."

She nodded and he smiled at her. They sat quietly then, staring at the street. A small bank of clean white fog drifted over the rooftops, dulling the sun for a moment. It was sheer and wispy and entirely beautiful. When it finally floated by, gently skimming along the blue sky, the sun seemed more golden, and the flowers in El Pintor's yard were as bright as jewels. She stole a quick glance at Rob and noticed with a little flurry of heartbeats how nicely his black hair grew and how strong his hands looked as they lay still on the arms of the chair.

In a few minutes, Rob said, "Guess I'd better be going." They both got up, and he added, "See you tomorrow then."

She nodded and he started down the steps. Then, because she felt guilty at having made him feel bad, she called, "Thanks. That'll be great."

He paused at the bottom of the steps, looked up at her, and smiled. "Tomorrow," he said.

She watched him leave, then went inside, wondering at her feelings. She had had dates before. For a short time last year she had even gone steady. That had been fun. Her steady, Richard, was a student at Halstead Academy, a boys' school at the other end of the small green valley in Virginia, where Raeburn was. Yes, it had been fun. Telephone calls, e-mail letters, secret messages on their beepers, and a date every weekend. Sure, there had been a few kisses and a tingle or two, but nothing more than that. Richard was a very proper young man and she—well, she hadn't really cared whether she kissed him or not.

So what was different about Rob? He was older, yes, and so was she, and maybe feelings did deepen as you grew older. Although that wasn't true of everybody. Look at the funk Courtney, her boarding school roomie, had fallen into when she and Greg broke up. Courtney really had been hurting.

For the rest of the afternoon and evening, thoughts of Rob, the way he looked, the way he talked, especially the way he'd smiled and said "Tomorrow" when he'd left, slid in and around the ordinary things she did. She talked to Laurita about El Pintor as they fixed supper together and washed the dishes. After flipping from channel to channel, Laurita and she agreed that Saturday-night TV was boring, and they chose an early bedtime.

Monica was sure that all the turmoil and excitement of the day would keep her awake. She was even more convinced of it when scenes from the day—walking on Parkview in the bright sun, meeting the Callahans, watching El Pintor at his bookcase, sitting on the porch with Rob— kept shifting and reforming in her mind like a kaleidoscope. Still, she was sleeping soundly when a voice awakened her.

"Courtney," she mumbled. "Courtney, wake up. You're talking in your sleep again." When the talking continued, she sat up. "Courtney," she started, then realized she was alone in her room in the house with Lucia. But there was a voice. Actually, there were two voices, and the sound of their whispering came through her open window.

"Dumb. You're as dumb as a mop. I said cans of *spray* paint."

Monica knew that voice. She'd heard it earlier that afternoon. Josie.

"It's all I could get," Licha answered. "But I brought brushes."

"All right, all right," Josie said. "It's gonna take longer, so get those cans open. We'll do the old man's house and then go for the car."

By this time Monica was out of bed and at the window. By pressing her head against the window frame, she could make out the dark forms of the two girls crouching near the front of the passage between the studio and the house. And their intentions were clear. Before they did something awful with their paint and brushes, she had to stop them. But how? Should she call the police? No, not the police. By the time they got here, the damage would be done. Monica's shoulders drooped. On Parkview, all she would have had to do was call the security patrol. For a moment she felt completely helpless. Then Josie's jeering face pushed into her mind, and she was furious. There was something she could do. Her dad's bedroom window was right above the two girls. She could throw a pail of water over them, just as if they were two brawling dogs. But would that discourage them or just make them madder? Then she had a better thought.

She ran through the house to the back door. Outside, with the help of a fading moon, she found the water hose connected to the faucet by the steps where Laurita had left it. Monica turned on the water, and the hose took on a life of its own, snaking across the yard, its nozzle shooting a long stream of water. Her heart pounded as she chased the squirming hose, her bare feet both wet and muddy. She picked up the hose, squeezed it together to stop the stream of water just as she had seen Laurita do. Then, with mud squeezing between her toes, she padded to the corner of the house.

She held her breath as she glanced around the wall. It would not have surprised her to find that, having heard the noises of the hose and the water, the girls had gone. But they were still there, bending over the paint cans, obviously having trouble removing the lids. Then Josie said, "There, that did it. Where are the brushes? Hurry."

Josie had pushed herself off the ground when Monica stepped into the open, aimed the nozzle, and let the water go. The force of the water caught Josie in the back, forcing her down on her hands and knees.

"What the—!" Josie shouted. "Dammit, what do you think you're doing!"

Licha threw her hands up to cover her face. "Stop it!" she wailed. "You're getting us all wet!"

Monica didn't stop. She couldn't. I've got a tiger by the tail, she thought. What'll happen if I do stop?

Josie grunted and tried to heave herself off the ground. She cursed loudly as she slipped in the watery mud. Then, as she struggled to right herself, she slipped once more and tipped over one of the paint cans.

"Oh, my God," Licha groaned. "There goes my father's paint. He'll kill me."

"I'm gonna kill you first and that bitch with the water, too!" Josie hollered. She turned to yell something at Monica and got a mouthful of water. "Sto-o-op!" she screeched.

As if her yell had been a signal, the lights went on in the studio and in Laurita's room.

"Laurita!" Monica shouted. "Call the police! These two are breaking and entering, disturbing the peace, and maliciously destroying property!" Afterwards, when she recalled this ridiculous list of charges, Monica would laugh. But, ridiculous or not, for now they did the trick. Josie and Licha, leaving the paint behind them, crawled toward the street and out of range of the hose. There they pushed themselves upright and ran awkwardly in the direction of Licha's house, Josie shouting obscenities over her shoulder.

Monica was turning off the water by the back steps when Laurita, in a flowered cotton nightgown, her feet bare, ran out the kitchen door. El Pintor, still dressed as he had been that afternoon, appeared from the back door of the studio.

"So the girls returned, did they?" he said, glancing down the passageway between the houses.

"They sure did," Monica answered.

Laurita said, "What a mess." She patted Monica's shoulder. "But not as bad as it might have been. You used your head, *chiquita.*"

Chapter Thirteen

The next morning, Sunday, Monica, Laurita, and El Pintor cleaned up the mud and paint in the passageway. The night before, the three of them had put away the half-emptied cans and the brushes. Sopa had appeared from nowhere and watched the nighttime activity with cautious interest from the safety of the back steps. Monica threw Sopa a glance. "Showing off how smart you are," she said under her breath. "You knew right away El Pintor was back, didn't you?" When they were done with the paints and the brushes, Laurita suggested that they drive "the Beemer" (she learned quickly) onto the front lawn close to the porch and that they leave the bright porch light on.

César arrived at Monica's back door bright and early that morning. "I figured you'd need my help," he said. "My mother and father think I'm at church, but I figured helping you is just as good."

Laurita raised her eyebrow. "It is? *Bueno, bueno.* We're about through with breakfast. How good are you at washing dishes?"

César shook his head vigorously. *"Not dishes!* I mean the paint mess."

"The paint?" Monica asked swiftly. "How did you know about that?"

"Easy," César said with a grin. "Everybody knows at my house. We all woke up because Licha was howling, Papá was shouting and my mother was crying—and praying. Well, praying doesn't make any noise, but I know she was because she always does. Anyway, that's how I know." His black eyes widened as he added, "Licha really got it. Papá gets kinda mean sometimes."

For the briefest of moments Monica felt sorry for Licha. But that feeling was quickly traded for annoyance at the fact that César knew what had gone on here the night before. César, she was sure, would tell the story to everyone he saw on Lucia, and, without knowing the reason why, she knew that the prospect of that made her extremely uncomfortable. But had she really expected to keep it secret? She shrugged and turned to Laurita. "Maybe," she said, averting her eyes from César's because she knew her impish intent would show in them, "maybe César could carry the paint cans back to his house. I heard Licha say they were her father's."

César stared at her for an instant. "Not me," he said, edging toward the back door. "I gotta get to church." He flung open the door and raced down the steps.

A few minutes after César's abrupt departure, the telephone rang. Monica hurried to it and was surprised at her disappointment when she heard her father's voice. In the ten or twelve steps it took to get from the kitchen to the hallway, she had convinced herself it would be Rob at the other end of the line.

"Dad," she said, trying to show enthusiasm, "how are you? It's about time you called."

"I called yesterday, honey. Laurita told me where you were. Didn't she mention it?"

"I guess. But, in all the excitement of finding El Pintor, I completely forgot." And also in the excitement of an almost graffiti attack, she thought, making a decision not to tell him until later.

"You found him?" her father said. "That *is* news. Tell me about it."

Quickly, she gave him the details of their search and their return home. "He still can't remember anything," she ended. "It's kind of sad."

"These things take time. Don't be impatient."

"You sound like Laurita."

"Well, that's not all bad, is it? Look, honey, I'll call you again tomorrow and let you know how things are going at my end."

Monica hung up. From the kitchen came the clink and clang of dishes and pans. Laurita was cleaning up the breakfast mess. She went in to help her. After they did the dishes, Laurita said that she was going to church and that Monica was welcome to go with her, if she wanted. Monica thanked

her and said no, and later watched Laurita's little Volkswagen tear down the street. She stood at the door, taking in the
Sunday silence. Oh, there were sounds, all right—voices in
the house next door, a screen door closing, a church bell
ringing—but they were hushed and sleepy. Even the birds'
songs seemed muted and serene. She wondered if most people on Lucia made a habit of going to church on Sunday.
Her father had never insisted that she go, but Rosa, shocked
at his casualness, had smuggled her into mass as often as
she could. At Raeburn, Courtney and she never attended
chapel; instead, they slept. She wondered about Rob and
decided he was probably sleeping. After all, moving a
refrigerator must have been a tiring job.

As she watched, two women came out of the house next
door. They wore bright summer dresses and high-heeled
pumps and tapped briskly past her house toward Dennison.
They were followed by two little girls, both in pink dresses,
pink socks, and sandals. Everyone, it seemed, had somewhere to go. She felt at loose ends. After the excitement of
Saturday, the hours of this day stretched out long and empty.

In a moment she closed the door and went to make her
bed. She threw back the blankets, but instead of going on
with the bed-making, stretched out on the floor to check on
the coffee can that held El Pintor's letter. It was there, back
in the far corner where she had pushed it. She made a reach-
ing movement toward it and then drew her hand back. No.
As much as she wanted to read that letter, she had to wait

until she talked to El Pintor. His memory *had* to return soon. Hadn't the doctors said so? In any case, it was good to know that the letter in its rusty old can was still there. She grimaced as she saw the dust bunnies around it. Their message was loud and clear: it was time to run a vacuum and use a dust cloth.

Rosa had taught her how to clean, even though it had never been a real responsibility. But now somebody's got to do it, she thought, and went looking for cleaning supplies. By the time Laurita returned from church, Monica had dusted and vacuumed her father's bedroom and hers and the living and dining rooms.

Laurita threw up her hands in mock surprise. "You've been cleaning," she said. "You must have known you were going to have company."

"I am? Who?"

"Toni. She's talking to El Pintor at his door. She waved and said she'd be right over."

The first thing Toni said when Monica opened the door for her was, "He doesn't remember anything or anybody! Not even Sopa."

Toni's face was so mournful, her voice so broken that Monica hurried to comfort her. "It's not as bad as all that," she said. "In a funny kind of way he remembered me."

"Yeah, I heard. Cristina. A lot of good that does." Toni stepped inside. "Anyway, that was way back when. I want him to remember *me* now."

Laurita, at the kitchen door, said, "*No le busques tres pies al gato,* Toni."

Toni laughed. "I never could figure out that old dicho. What do you mean, 'Don't look for three paws on a cat?'"

"Come on, come on," Laurita said. "I thought you'd grown up with these sayings. It means, don't look for what isn't so or is not possible. So, have patience. He'll remember all of us eventually."

"Except me," Monica said. "He didn't ever know me."

"He knew you as a baby," Laurita said. "He'll remember you, all right." She disappeared into the kitchen.

"It's strange," Toni said with a sad shake of her head. "All my life El Pintor's been there. He helped everybody on Lucia. When someone needed something translated or if there was a form to fill out, everyone went to him. Even with homework. Just last month he helped me with a paper for English Comp. Funny. He's here, but he really isn't."

"That must feel weird."

"It sure does." Toni shrugged in a resigned way. "Oh, well. He looked relieved when I told him I knew where he kept everything. Papers, and all that stuff. I'm going over later to show him."

Toni plopped down on the couch and looked around the room. "Hey, this place sure looks different than when the Valenzuelas were here. You know, your last renters? But I guess you *wouldn't* know. El Pintor took care of all that, didn't he?"

"I guess." She sat on a chair facing Toni. She tucked her legs under her and said, "Were you friends with the people who lived here?"

"Kind of. They had a daughter about my age. Teresa. I thought we'd be friends, but pretty soon I found out she had some dumb ideas. She wanted us to start a girls' gang. At first it sounded like it might be fun. You know, like a club of our very own. And then she showed me her collection of . . . of stuff. She had a pair of the ugliest-looking knives you ever saw, some heavy rocks in a long sock—she had a name for that; I don't remember what—and, would you believe it, a gun?" Toni shook her head as she went on. "Even Rob, when he belonged to a gang, didn't have anything like that."

Monica's attention sharpened. So Rob had belonged to a gang. A gang out of which El Pintor had undoubtedly pulled him. "How long was Rob in a gang?" she asked.

"Long enough to turn my mother's hair white, so she says. So no way, even if I'd wanted to, was I going to get into one. Terry—Teresa, that is—blew up when I told her. She had other girls lined up, including César's sister, Licha, but it seems it was *me* she wanted. Go figure."

"That's not hard," Monica said. "She was after Rob."

"Maybe," Toni said, giving her a sharp little glance. "What Terry really wanted was to go after The Green Street Gang. That's where she'd lived before, and the guys there wouldn't let her in with them. So she was going to show them how tough a girls' gang could be. It didn't happen, though. Next thing we knew Licha was sent for a long visit to her cousins in Mexico, and the Valenzuelas, after living here only six months, moved away." Toni looked out the front window for a few seconds. She turned back to Monica and said, "I don't think all that just happened, if you know what I mean. I think someone kept an eye on what was going on and pulled a few strings."

"Who? Sounds like coincidence to me."

"Maybe. All I know is that my father says that when he was growing up, El Pintor used to sit outside on that bench of his for hours at a time. Like he was keeping watch on the street and the kids. I haven't noticed him sitting on those benches lately, but I know he sits at that table by his front window a lot." Toni shrugged. "Who knows?"

"Right," Monica echoed, "who knows?" And then, "The closest thing to a gang I ever belonged to was my Girl Scout troop. They weren't wild like Josie or your friend Terry, but just as crazy. We were all just about thirteen when I left for Washington, and two of the girls were already into pot. About a year later Candice—she was the smartest and prettiest of all of us—ran away from home and was missing for a couple of weeks. I was gone already, so I don't know how that ended."

They were silent for a moment, and then Toni said, "I guess we grew up in two different kinds of places. Except that, in some ways, they aren't all that different."

Monica found it hard to say anything to that. Maybe kids did get into trouble all over, but neighborhoods weren't alike. Certainly, this sad little street was nothing like Parkview.

"Talking about problems," Toni said, "I hear you gave Josie a bath last night."

Monica grinned. "Not a very nice one, but it was that or have the studio and my dad's car trashed. Which reminds me, where's the nearest car wash? The one you all use, I mean."

Toni looked at her with surprise, then said good-humoredly, "The nearest car wash is the hose you used last night. The ones we all use are attached to our houses. Most people on Lucia can't afford to waste money on car washes."

Monica swung her legs out from under her and placed them firmly on the floor. "I see. Or waste money on moving refrigerators either. I got a sermon on that last night."

"That had to be Rob," Toni said. "Don't pay any attention to him. Or to me." She leaned toward Monica. "Besides, it's easy to wash a car. Grab some rags and let's go do it."

"Would you?" Monica jumped up. "I'll go see what rags Rosa left us. They're in the back porch." She was already in the dining room, Toni close at her heels, when there was a loud knocking at the front door.

"That sounds like trouble," Toni said.

"Why? It's probably just César with more neighborhood news."

"Uh-uh. Kids on Lucia know to use the back doors. Sounds like an angry neighbor to me."

Monica walked quickly to the front door and swung it open. Standing there was a short, barrel-chested man. He had thick, unkempt gray hair, and his face, with a day's growth of beard, was set and serious. Hiding behind him stood a limp, worn-looking Licha.

Chapter Fourteen

"I have business with your father," the man boomed, and his voice bounced off the living room walls. "Call him."

Licha edged to the man's side and tugged at his sleeve. "*No, Papá, no es—*" she began, but her father thrust her hand away from his arm and she shrank behind him once more.

Monica, too, took a step away from the man at the door. "I'm sorry, sir," she said. "My father isn't home. But when he comes back, I'll tell him you were here."

The man shook his head impatiently and muttered something that she couldn't make out. Behind her, Toni giggled softly and whispered, "It's an angry neighbor, all right."

The man frowned at Monica. "Then tell your mother," he barked.

"My mother is—" Monica started, but Laurita's words interrupted.

"Señor Gámez," she was saying as she hurried from the kitchen, "what is this? What do you want with this girl?"

"With her, nothing. It's her parents I came to speak to."

"Well, then," Laurita said, "since neither of her parents is here, I will have to do." By this time she had pressed Monica aside and was confronting the man. "Come in, come in," she added, pushing open the screen door. "What do you want?"

"No, no," Señor Gámez said, a bit more pleasantly, "we won't come in. This will be quick." He pulled Licha forward. "María Luisa wishes to apologize to you for her actions last night."

"María Luisa?" Monica whispered to Toni.

"That's Licha," Toni whispered back. "You know, a nickname."

Laurita put her arm around Monica and said, "I think she needs to apologize to Monica. This is Monica's home."

Laurita's gesture, Monica knew, was a kind and generous one, but she wished she hadn't made it. She wanted to shout, please leave me out of this! This isn't my home. I'm only here temporarily. The screen door was still open, and a fly buzzed in and circled around her head, adding to her discomfort. Angrily, she brushed it away.

Licha, meanwhile, had moved up a step. With her eyes staring at the porch floor, she said, "I'm sorry we bothered you last night."

"*What?*" her father shouted.

Licha drew in her breath and shuddered. "I'm sorry we made such a mess," she muttered.

"*And?*"

Licha glanced at Monica, then down at the floor again. "I'm sorry we spilled paint on your side yard," she said, the words squeezing through tight lips.

"*María Luisa!*" Señor Gámez bellowed.

Licha swallowed hard and, with her voice hardly above a whisper, said, "I'm sorry for the evil things we planned to do." She glanced at her father and went on. "I'll be glad to help with your housework, or whatever you want, to make up for all the trouble I caused."

Monica spoke quickly. "No, no, Señor Gámez. She doesn't have to do that."

Licha's father ignored Monica and spoke to Laurita. "What time do you want her to come?"

Laurita looked at Monica with a question and Monica shrugged. "Come at nine o'clock, Licha," Laurita said. "And, Señor Gámez, your paints—what's left of them—are in a box by the back door."

"Get them, María Luisa," her father said, and Licha, blinking back tears, went down the porch steps.

"I'll see that she gets here," Señor Gámez said and followed his daughter down the steps.

"How do you like that?" Toni said. She swung around in a full circle. "Too bad there's nothing to do here. It looks like somebody just cleaned."

"Somebody *did* just clean," Monica said. "Me. I wish I'd known."

Toni giggled. Monica took one look at Toni and burst into laughter. Toni said, "What's so funny?" and they both laughed harder.

Monica said, "Nothing, nothing at all." But she choked on the last syllable, and that made them wail with laughter so unpredictable and uncontrollable that they bent over, hugging their abdomens. Their laughter finally subsided.

"*Bueno,*" Laurita said from the kitchen door, "what's this all about? Am I missing something?"

"No," Monica said, struggling up from the floor, "but we are. Some of our marbles. Now, cut it out, Toni. I can't laugh anymore. Besides, I'm hungry. Do you want a sandwich?"

Toni stayed for lunch. Soon after she left, Laurita left to visit with her brother's family. "I'll just be gone for a couple of hours," she had said. "I wish you'd come with me. My brother's wife especially asked me to invite you. She says you won't be bored; there's always a lot of coming and going at her house and, if you want, lots of guitar music."

Monica had thanked her for her second invitation of the day and said she thought she'd stay home. Maybe she'd write a letter to Courtney. "Don't rush back, Laurita," she had insisted. "I'll be fine. I'll see you when I see you." When she had gone, Monica sat down to write to Courtney and found that she had nothing to say. What would Courtney care about a mysterious letter found in the attic, or a missing old man called El Pintor, or even how they'd searched and found him? Even a phone call probably would bore Courtney. If she was being unfair to Courtney, if it was her mood coloring her thinking, it was just as well to wait for a better mood to write or talk to her. Once she had made that decision and pushed paper and her favorite pen aside, she found that the minutes dragged and that the house felt dismally empty.

It was not that she wasn't used to being alone. Her home had never been filled with people or activity. Quiet hours were not strange to her, but today there was something unquiet about the house. There was a waiting restlessness in the air, the kind of prickly restlessness that as a little kid, she had endured on Fourth of July and Halloween. It had seemed then that those nights of tingling excitement would never come. With that thought she caught her breath. So that was it. She couldn't wait for tonight to come. And she had tried to hide that eagerness from herself. But she should have known. Her constant glances at the telephone should have told her.

Come on now, Monica, she told herself, cut it out. Rob's a nice guy, but he's not Prince Charming. (Nor would I want him to be, a little voice said within her, but she ignored it.) It's only a date. What you need is to get your mind on something else. What you need is a book.

She had learned a book's value early in life. "There's no reason for any intelligent person to be bored," her dad had scolded her when she complained of nothing to do, "not as long as there are books to be read." Today, most of their books were still in storage, but there were two or three boxes packed with books, some hers, some her dad's, in a corner of the garage. Her dad had assured her that although the garage was primarily for El Pintor's use, they had permission from him to store some things in there. So she hurried through the house to the service porch, picked up the garage key, and went outside.

The padlock on the garage door opened easily, but the half of the large double door that she pulled toward her did not. The hinges on it creaked resentfully as she urged it outward, so, once there was an opening wide enough for her to slip through, she stopped tugging at it. A shaft of sunlight fell into the garage. She followed it inside. As she did, something grazed the top of her head. She gave a little gasp, but good sense came to her aid immediately. She took a step back and looked above her. Just as in her bedroom closet, a long string with a ceramic weight hung from a light bulb attached to a cross board below the ceiling. When she pulled the string, the darkness disappeared, revealing wood and tar paper walls above neatly stacked canvases. There was a worktable in the center of the room that held what looked like wooden picture frames. Perhaps from that table or from the years-old pine of the walls and ceiling came a sweet, woodsy smell.

The canvases on their light wood frames were placed on redwood blocks that kept them off the floor. Toni is right, she thought; El Pintor really loves his paintings. Her gaze circled the room. The paintings were stacked against all three walls except in one corner in the back. There, four or five cardboard boxes took up the space. The box with her books and papers, including two new paperbacks she had been given for her birthday, was on the floor and easily accessible. All she had to do now was cut through that clear mailing tape that she knew would be as firmly set as indelible ink. She scanned the room for help and gave thanks when she saw a knife on the worktable beside the picture frames.

Monica put the knife on the floor beside the boxes and edged her carton away from the others. She wanted it closer to the light. As she jockeyed the box forward, one side bumped into the row of canvases beside it, forcing the top painting to fall to its side and unsettling the dark plastic that covered it. She picked up the plastic, straightened the painting, and paused to look at it.

It was of a dark-haired woman standing by a cement pillar that was topped by a carved urn. The pillar was one of two at the entrance to a large, tree-shaded house, the upper story of which could be seen through the trees in the background. The dark green of the leaves, the russet tone of the house, the grays of the road and the pillar were muted. It was the woman who, although wearing a plain white dress whose only ornament was a heart-shaped pin at the neckline, brightened the picture. Monica studied the canvas. Was

it the woman's smile, a hesitant little smile that seemed about to disappear, that made her so appealing? Maybe. All I know, Monica thought as she brought the plastic cover over the frame, is that she's a lovely lady to look at. She turned her attention to her box of books, but her glance kept straying to the dark plastic cover and the picture it hid.

When she was back in the house, a couple of books in hand, her thoughts, too, returned to the painting. There was something familiar about the lady in white. Not that she'd ever seen her before, she was sure of that. But there was a feeling of knowing her. Maybe, she thought, she reminds me of one of my teachers—maybe Mrs. Ross, my kindergarten teacher, because she seems to be someone I knew long ago when I was very young.

With the help of an exciting mystery novel, the rest of the afternoon passed quickly for Monica. Laurita came home, and together they prepared a dinner of leftover cold chicken, fruit salad with fresh peaches, and hot buttered corn tortillas that Laurita had brought home from her brother's. They were just through eating when the phone rang. Monica, who had forgotten to listen for its ring in the last couple of hours, now raced to it, leaving a smiling Laurita in the kitchen. It was Rob. Was seven okay? And what movie would she like to see? Sure, he'd be glad to pick one, but don't blame him if she didn't like it.

Right on the dot at seven, Rob's pickup, clean if not shiny, drove up before Monica's house. Monica, who was

sitting on a chair on the front porch, got to her feet, disturbing Sopa who had been sleeping beside her. She called
goodbye to Laurita and climbed into the truck beside Rob.

"You look nice," Rob said.

"Thanks," Monica replied. She was glad that, after putting it on and taking it off several times, she had finally
worn the blue striped sundress. She wanted to say, you look
nice, too, because he did, and also that he smelled good, like
soap and after-shave, but she couldn't get the words out.
She busied herself straightening out the seat belt, then
looked up and said, "Did you pick a movie?"

"Didn't dare," he said with a grin. "But I brought the
movie section of the paper. It's on the floor beside you."

Monica picked it up. "Maybe we should both look at it,"
she said as they drove by César's house. She waved to César
who was sitting on his front steps eating an ice-cream cone.
They were at the end of the block now, and Rob pulled the
truck around, stopping it at the foot of the road that led to
the top of the overgrown hill where she had first bumped
into Licha and Josie.

"Okay," Rob said, spreading out the paper across the
dashboard, "here are the choices." The paper crackled as he
smoothed it out. "Monica," he said, touching her arm, "I
said here, not up on Chimney Hill."

She frowned as she turned back to him. "Sorry. It's just
that . . ." She paused, thinking, *it's just that what?* "Rob,"

she said, "could we walk up the hill for a minute? There's something up there I want to look at."

"On Chimney Hill? Nothing's up there but the remains of an old house that burned down a million—well, a long time ago. All that's left is part of three chimneys. They must've really been built because they're still standing after a couple of earthquakes."

"What about the pillars at the entrance? Didn't they belong to the house?"

"The pillars at the front? Oh, yeah, sure. I forgot about them."

"They're what I want to see," Monica said, tugging at the door. "I'll only be a minute." As she jumped down to the ground, she heard the car door slam on the other side.

"I'm coming with you," Rob said, striding around the back of the pickup. "Everybody says there are ghosts up there."

"I'll bet," Monica said. "Like Licha and her friend Josie. They're the ghosts I saw here a couple of days ago." She smiled. "And they came to haunt El Pintor and me last night."

"I heard," Rob said, angling a grin at her. "And I heard how you scared them off."

"I think I was more scared than they were."

They walked on the cracked and weed-grown asphalt until they were at the top of the slope and near the vine-grown pillars. Monica walked up to one and picked her way slowly around it. Here and there under the ivy she saw bits of the beige and rose-hued stones that made up the solid columns. She scrunched up her face and angled her head as she looked up at the bird-spattered, ivy-covered broken adornment that topped it. "If it wasn't all hidden by the ivy, I'd be sure, but I think . . ." She paused, then pointing to the top of the pillar, she said, "Rob, what do you think that thing up there is?"

"That's easy. One of those Greek vases."

"An urn? That's what I thought." She stared thoughtfully at the pillars, then took a few steps under the overhanging trees toward the crumbling walls that outlined the house. "Do you mind if I look around a little more?"

Rob shrugged. "Sure. I mean, no. But why? What're you looking for?"

"I don't know. Nothing, I guess. It's the pillars I wanted to see. They're in a painting of El Pintor's that was done when the house was still here and the birds and the ivy hadn't done a job on them."

Rob looked surprised. "That had to be a long time ago. I didn't know he'd been around then. Sure it was this place?"

She nodded briskly. "Yes. Even the trees are the same. But I suppose I could be wrong. Tell you what. If you're not in a hurry, let's go back and look at the painting. You'll see what I mean."

"Sure. I guess that's okay." He looked disappointed for a moment, then his look changed as he studied her face. "Why are you so interested in El Pintor? You only met him yesterday. If it's because he thought you were Cristina, there's nothing strange about that. He lived right next door to her all those years when she was growing up. And you look like her."

She shook her head. "It's not that."

"Then what?"

"I don't really know," she said hesitantly. She couldn't tell him about the letter to her mother waiting in the old coffee can beneath her bed. She couldn't tell him that she wanted El Pintor's permission to read that letter. But even if she could, what did *this* have to do with *that?* "I don't know," she repeated, and this time her words had a ring of truth. "Maybe it's because I love a mystery, and he's one. Where did he come from? Why did my grandparents, and my mother, too, let him live in the studio for free? And what was he doing in my old neighborhood, sketching all those places I knew so well? And now, this. What did he have to do with the house that used to stand here? Because, Rob, the more I look around, the more I'm sure it's the one I saw in the painting."

Rob patted her arm. "To heck with the movie. Come on, let's go."

Laurita was outside when they drove up. "I've been talking with El Pintor," she said as they went into the house.

"What a good man he is. What patience. So, why are you back so soon? What did you forget?"

"It's not what I forgot," Monica answered. "More like what I think I remembered." She told Laurita about the painting she'd seen and how she was going to show it to Rob and then they could both compare the pillars in the painting to those on Chimney Hill. "I meant to tell you about it before," she finished, "but I got so involved in my book that I forgot to."

Laurita said, "I'd like to see that painting, too."

"Good," Monica said, "maybe you'll remember the lady."

Laurita smiled and shook her head. "Maybe, but I doubt it. I think that old place burnt down when I was just a baby—and that was a million years ago."

Rob grinned. "Just like I told you."

Outside, Rob pulled the sticky garage door open wide, and the daylight filled the dark corners. Monica uncovered the painting.

Laurita looked at it for a few minutes, then nodded and said, "That must be the house that was on Chimney Hill. My mother used to tell long stories about what a special place it was, how the trees shaded the beautiful gardens, and how this whole neighborhood had been planned to be a place of big, elegant houses. I used to think she was dressing up the story, but I guess not."

"Do you suppose she was, just a little?" Rob said. "There are a lot of grungy shacks on this street that go back a long, long time."

"Oh, that was no problem for my mother," Laurita said with a laugh. "She had an answer for that. All the old houses were going to be torn down. And, as you know, a few *did* come down up the street toward the hill. Unless those just fell apart from a creaky old age."

Rob said, "Well, dressed up or not, it's the same story my grandmother told. She said everything came to an end when the big house on the hill burned down under mysterious circumstances."

"Mysterious?" Monica asked. "Why?"

Rob shrugged. "Who knows? But that's how the ghost business got started."

Laurita said, "All the old-timers seem to have a version of why it was mysterious, but none of their stories agree, and no one seems to have any real facts." She smiled. "*Cada loco con su tema.* And don't ask what that means, Monica. You figure it out."

"Sounds like, 'Every wacko with his own theme,'" Monica said, and Laurita answered, "Close enough."

Monica looked back at the woman in the painting. The faint feeling of familiarity tugged at her. "I wonder if she was around when it happened," she said softly. Laurita, too, was looking at the painting, her smile still lingering. Then the smile disappeared and her eyes narrowed as she focused on one spot in the picture. She turned when Monica spoke.

"Well, another mystery to unravel," she said.

"Don't unravel too much too soon," Laurita said in a somber tone. "You may get the threads twisted. Wait for El Pintor. He'll be able to answer your questions."

Monica looked at her with surprise. What had changed Laurita's mood? Still, Laurita was right. El Pintor would undoubtedly have simple and logical explanations for all the things that seemed so puzzling now. Except . . . except for the letter under her bed that her mother had never read. How could the explanation for that be simple? And could El Pintor explain away this feeling of recognition of someone that—given the time frame—she obviously could never have known?

She was still wondering about that as they locked the garage and went into the house. Suddenly the dark and dingy garage, the painting and the pillars, the questions and the guesses, were no fun. They were more like an interruption, a telephone call in the middle of a favorite TV show. She could have been watching a good movie with Rob, and instead, here she was poking into the past, into things that probably had nothing to do with her. Well, she had no one to blame but herself, so if she wanted things to change, it was up to her. She put the key away in the back porch cupboard and went into the living room.

Rob was standing in the center of the room. He started to say something, then changed his mind. He looked uncomfortable, she thought, like a little kid in grownup company trying to find something polite to say.

"Hey," she said quickly, "I'm sorry about the movie. My curiosity got the better of me—big time."

"No problem," Rob said. "Maybe we could go for a ride or something."

"Something," Monica said decisively. "Like a trip to the nearest Blanchard's for a latte or a mocha something and a piece of triple-rich chocolate cake. Comfort food. On me."

"No way," Rob said. "Wherever we go, I buy. It won't be a Blanchard's though. Not around here. But there's Amelia's Café on Dennison. She makes the best pies and cakes you've ever eaten." He looked at his watch. "She closes at nine-thirty, so we can make it."

"That sounds good," Monica said. "Laurita," she called into the hall, "we're gone again."

They stepped out onto the porch. The summer twilight had deepened into night, and in the southern sky an early star blinked hesitantly. The air was cooler and had a touch of ocean mist. And from a neighboring house came the sound of music, a plaintive love ballad, and cheerful voices.

"It's a pretty night, isn't it?" Monica said, and Rob nodded and smiled at her. She breathed in deeply. As they walked to the pickup and climbed into its cab, the scent of El Pintor's flowers seemed to follow them.

Rob put the key in the ignition, but didn't turn it. He pulled his hand away and looked at Monica. "Let's begin our date again," he said. "You look awfully nice."

This time Monica found the words, but she looked straight ahead as she said them. "So do you. And I like your after-shave."

When she felt Rob's hand on her cheek, she turned and smiled. She raised her face to meet his. When she felt his mouth on hers, she sighed and let her arms slide around his neck.

After a few minutes, Rob leaned back and said, "Do you still want chocolate cake?"

Monica pushed him away lightly. "Sure, I do," she said. "Nothing ever takes the place of chocolate cake."

Chapter Fifteen

That night Monica had a dream, a dream in which Rob and she walked hand in hand up Chimney Hill past the stone columns, on to stepping stones that led through a brilliant mass of low-growing flowers to a wide front door. The rest of the house was obscured by clouds that billowed and swirled restlessly just above their heads. They knocked on the massive door, and it was thrown open by El Pintor. Standing behind him in an entryway lighted by a blazing chandelier was the dark-haired woman from the painting. The same little half smile came and went on her lips as she beckoned to them and said, "Come in, come in. We've been waiting for you." As she spoke, the hovering clouds surged through the doorway, taking the house, El Pintor, and the lady in white away with them in a burst of dizzying energy and leaving Rob and Monica alone in a cold gray mist on the crest of Chimney Hill.

Finally, Monica was awake enough to realize that the sadness, the emptiness she felt, was leftover from the dream. She sat up, punched her goose-feather pillow into a more comfortable shape and, with pleasant thoughts of Rob and chocolate cake, went back to sleep.

The dream was quickly forgotten the next morning when Licha, true to her word, or maybe that of her father, arrived promptly at nine. She was dressed more somberly than before: blue denim shorts and a white T-shirt. Her garish sandals were replaced by well-worn white sneakers that hid the black varnish of her toenails.

Monica looked at her with suspicion. Maybe, she thought, Licha has toned down her clothes to impress her father only. Not that I blame her. But we'll see if her attitude matches them. Laurita had put Licha to work on the side yard with an old broom and a rake. And, although Licha did what she was asked with no word of complaint, Monica could see that her eyes were filled with resentment.

Monica was feeling resentment, too. She was uncomfortable about the whole thing. If Licha's father wanted his daughter to make amends, well, then he should be seeing to it. I know Licha owes us something. I know she needs to make up for the mess Josie and she made, and the worse mess that they might have made, but . . . but no way should we be in charge of her punishment. After half an hour of moving restlessly from room to room, peeking through the windows at Licha's determined, though listless, progress, Monica felt worse. There ought to be something we can do, she thought, and went looking for Laurita.

When she couldn't find her in the house, she went to the front door to see if her VW was still there. Could she have gone somewhere and not told her? She opened the door and looked through the screen. The little car was there. Well, then, where was Laurita? Feeling more annoyed than perplexed, she pushed open the screen door and stepped outside. Immediately, she heard voices. They came from the side yard.

"It looked like a flower to me." Licha was speaking. "Isn't it?"

"Yes, it's a flower." That was El Pintor. "A little volunteer from the—from my garden. An impatiens."

"It's too pretty for such a funny name," Licha said.

Monica hurried down the steps and turned the corner of the house. As she did, Laurita appeared from the backyard, a hoe and a spade in her hands. She went directly to El Pintor.

"I borrowed these from your shed, Señor Mead," she said. "I thought I'd give Licha a hand."

"Me, too," Monica called and suddenly felt better.

"Well," El Pintor said, adjusting the white cap on his head, "I also need a bit of exercise, so it looks as if this young lady will have a lot of help."

Licha rubbed her hands on her denim shorts and turned to look, not at El Pintor, but at Laurita. Her expression showed surprise, then disbelief. Finally, her eyes narrowed, and her forehead furrowed into lines of suspicion. "What're you gonna do?" she muttered, her eyes going from face to face. "Gang up on me?"

"Oh, sh—," Monica started, caught herself and said, "Oh, flip! Don't you ever think of anything but gangs?" She knew that the annoyance of the morning was slipping through in her words, but she didn't care. "Hasn't it ever occurred to you that there are people who like to be good to each other? Like El Pintor? Like Laurita? Maybe even me." She walked over to Laurita and held out her hand. "Okay, okay," she said, "give me that spade. We're here to garden, aren't we? Let's get on with it."

Laurita smiled widely. "Not so fast," she said, hanging on to the spade. "We have to talk about what we're going to do. We don't want to do anything your father would object to." She turned to speak to El Pintor, but said nothing as her smile changed into a puzzled frown.

El Pintor's deep blue eyes were fixed on Monica's face. "Cristina," he said sharply, "what is this?" He stopped and shook his head as if to dislodge something, then said slowly, painfully, "You're not Cristina. No. Cristina was not like that. She was timid, not outspoken. But if you're not Cristina, then who—" He gestured impatiently with unsteady hands, and the question floated unfinished in the soft morning air.

Monica blinked back tears, swallowed hard, and said, "I'm Monica, Mr. Mead, Monica Ramos." She threw a glance at Laurita, and Laurita returned a quick smile and a nod. "I live here," Monica added.

El Pintor ran his fingers through his thick white hair. "Yes, I know. Of course. Cristina lives . . . no, no, Cristina *lived* there. But . . ." He looked around at the three of them as if searching for an explanation. "Something happened, didn't it? Yes. She left here. She married. She married that young lawyer, and then . . . and then," he added simply, "she died."

Laurita's words were soft but firm. "That was a long time ago, Señor."

"It was?" There was the hint of an apology in El Pintor's smile. "I knew that, of course. Something's dulled my memory. Still, perhaps it's coming back to me now."

Monica held her breath. This was it. El Pintor's memory was returning! Another quick look at him told her that she had jumped too quickly to her happy conclusion. His smile could not hide the haunted look in his eyes.

He took a deep breath, let the air out slowly, and with obvious effort said, "So, young lady, you live next door, do you?"

"Yes. But I just came a few days ago." She paused, wondering if she should go on, and then because it seemed the right thing to do, she said, "I'm Cristina's daughter."

"Well," he said, nodding slowly, "so that was it." His expression now was unreadable, but there was a bite of anger in his voice as he added, "And I mistook you for her. Well, and why would I do that?"

"Because I look like her, of course," Monica said. There was an edge of irritation in her voice, too.

"You're not alone in that mistake, Señor Mead." Laurita said. "There are a lot of us who want to call her Cristina. Those of us who knew her mother, that is." She turned to the girls. "*Bueno,*" she said crisply, "let's get on with what we were doing."

"Yeah," Licha said, "like we know what. What are we doing, anyway?"

It was clear that for a moment Laurita didn't know how to take Licha's remark. Then, as if she couldn't help herself, she began to laugh. Monica looked at her, wondered what she was laughing at, shrugged, looked at her again, and, without knowing why, began to laugh, too.

Licha's face grew red.

El Pintor said, "They're not laughing at you, girl. They're laughing at themselves. That's right. It's time to lighten up. Look. The soil's nice and damp all the way to the front of the house." He threw Monica a look that held a touch of mischief, and she knew he was referring to the hosing-down she'd given it the night before. "I'll help dig it up, and we can plant flowers all along this side of the house. There are more volunteer impatiens, and you can get cuttings from your geraniums." He took the spade from Laurita. "Go on, go on, girls. Snip the geraniums, and I'll look for the plants you can dig up."

Licha mumbled something that sounded suspiciously like "crazies," and followed Laurita into the backyard.

A couple of hours later, the job was essentially done. Everyone had worked hard, snipping the right cuttings from the red geraniums, digging on their knees in the muddy ground, pulling the hose from one spot to the other, but no one worked as hard as El Pintor. He seemed to lose himself in turning over huge spadefuls of moist earth along the full length of the house. His lightened mood had disappeared as he worked in silence, his forehead furrowed in deep concentration.

Licha, who was digging in the ground beside him, kept giving him quick little glances, then turning away guiltily, as if she were eavesdropping on a private conversation.

Laurita, too, glanced at him occasionally, not with curiosity but with concern. Finally, she stepped back from the plantings and said, "I think we're about done. Don't you, Señor Mead?" When he nodded absently, she went on, "And wasn't this a good morning's work?"

He raised his head, stared at Laurita for a long moment, and said quickly, "Yes, yes, of course."

"We need something cold to drink" Laurita said. "*Vengan, muchachas,* help me make some lemonade."

El Pintor said, "Thank you. None for me. What I need . . . what I need . . ." He stopped and brushed the dirt off his hands slowly, almost deliberately. "No, no lemonade. I need to go in now." He muttered something more that was unintelligible, looked around as if for direction, then nodded and went to the studio's door.

When it had closed behind him, Licha pushed herself off the ground and said, "He's weird. And, hey, forget the lemonade for me. I told my father I'd work here an hour or so. A couple, max. And it's way past that now." She tossed the trowel she had been holding to the ground, and it clanged loudly as it fell against the metal spade. "So I'm through with the program. I'm going now. Okay?"

"Sure," Monica said and bit her lip to keep from adding, you're certainly brave when your father's not around.

When Licha reached the far end of the house, she stopped, stood still for a moment, then suddenly spun around. "I'll be back and see if the things grow," she called.

Monica shrugged. "They'll be sure to grow if Laurita's still here. But nothing grows for me. Even plastic flowers fade when I look at them."

"Yeah, I guess they would," Licha said and hurried around the corner of the house.

Laurita grinned at Monica and spread her arms out in a gesture of defeat. "Let's go get some lunch," she said.

Although the lemonade they made was sweet and tart and icy and the tuna sandwiches were crunchy with bits of celery and pickle and rich with mayonnaise, Monica didn't enjoy them. The problem was El Pintor. She couldn't get him out of her mind. Twice during the morning he had acted . . . well, to say the least, strangely. Could the bump on his head have caused more than amnesia?

Laurita, too, ate silently.

Monica swallowed the last gulp of her lemonade and said, "You're thinking about El Pintor, aren't you?"

Laurita sighed, then nodded. "Yes, I am. It's as if you— no, not you—Cristina was his anchor and losing her has left him floating in a boundless sea."

"I've been thinking about him, too." Monica moved her empty plate carefully to one side and leaned across the table. "But don't you think that maybe that was just what he needed? You know, like a slap in the face when someone's going bananas."

"But maybe this slap was too hard." Laurita gave her a wicked little grin. "Mashed bananas." Then she added seriously, "Maybe he shouldn't have worked so hard in the sun."

Monica jumped up from the table. "Let's go see him," she said. "Do we need an excuse? Well, even if we don't need one, let's throw together a tuna sandwich for him and some chips. He might not want enchiladas again. Come on, Laurita, let's do it. I'm worried about him, too."

"*Bueno, bueno,*" Laurita said and stood up. "I guess we should check on him."

In a matter of minutes, they were knocking on the studio's back door. As they waited, Monica heard a rustling sound above and behind them. Looking up, she found the cat Sopa poised at the edge of the garage roof. The orange and black patches of her multicolored coat glistened in the midday sunlight. She meowed a greeting and jumped gracefully down to the neighbor's fence and then to the ground beside them.

"She smells the tuna," Lauita said.

"Maybe. But maybe what she wants is to see El Pintor, too."

They knocked again. This time when they got no answer, Monica threw a quick look at Laurita and reached for the doorknob. She turned it firmly and, finding that the door was not locked, pushed it open. She started to step over the threshold but something—her childhood fear of trespassing?—held her back.

"It's all right," Laurita whispered and stepped in ahead of her. "Come on."

Monica closed the door behind her. "Mr. Mead," she called softly.

A quick scan of the high-ceilinged room showed them that El Pintor was not there. Except for some scattered papers on the worktable, everything was as Monica remembered it: the colorful paintings hung high on the walls; the work in progress on the nearest easel, still in blue and gray outline; the stack of paintings in the corner that held "Springtime." Both Laurita and she stood absolutely still, as if wondering what their next step should be.

As they hesitated, Sopa sped past them to the closed door in the forward wall. She let out a plaintive meow and when there was no response, crouched close to the floor and nudged the door with her head. It opened a crack and she slithered through it.

Sopa's done that before, Monica thought with a little shudder. What would Sopa find on the other side of the door? I'm being silly, she told herself, but whether I am or not, we've still got to look. "We can't just stand here," she whispered to Laurita, "can we? We've got to find him."

Laurita nodded and they started for the door. They were across the room and about to push it open when a voice stopped them. It was El Pintor's.

"Well, well, Sopa," he was saying. "Up to your old tricks, are you? Come in, girl, come in. Where have you been? I've missed you."

Chapter Sixteen

"He sounds all right," Monica whispered happily. "Should we go in?"

"Did you bring me company, Sopa?" El Pintor's voice reached them clearly. "I hear voices. Toni, is that you?"

Laurita said, "It's your next-door neighbors, Señor Mead."

"Monica and Laurita," Monica added, pushing the door open gently.

El Pintor was seated in a wicker chair that faced the door, his head resting on a cushion that matched two others on the couch-bed. His hair was tousled and his eyes were heavy; it was clear that he had just awakened. Sopa, who was on the floor carefully licking a raised paw, took a sudden leap, landing on El Pintor's lap. There she made two complete turns and then, purring steadily, settled herself across El Pintor's thighs.

El Pintor, adjusting himself for Sopa's comfort, looked up at them and said, "I'm afraid I've been asleep."

"Oh," Laurita said. "Forgive us for wakening you, Señor. We'll leave you to your nap."

"No, no. Come in. And forgive *me* for not rising, but the cat precludes that courtesy, eh?" He stroked Sopa's fur and added, "In any case I'm glad to be awakened. I've been having some strange dreams. Sit down, sit down, please."

Laurita quickly took a chair near El Pintor's, and Monica sank to a cushion on the floor beside her. She jumped up as quickly as she had sat down. "We brought you a sandwich, Mr. Mead," she said, holding out a paper sack. "And chips, too. What would you like me to do with them?"

"Thank you. Please just put them on the counter. As soon as I can get rid of the kitty, I'll get them. I woke up very hungry."

"You don't have to wait," Monica said. "I'll take her. Sopa and I are good friends." She placed the sack on the counter and knelt on the floor by El Pintor's knees. "Come on, Sopa," she said, scratching the cat behind its ears. "Come on, baby, come with me."

Sopa stood up, stretched, and jumped to the floor. Monica picked her up and went to a chair across the room, where she settled her on her lap.

El Pintor shook his head. "Now I believe in miracles. She's never gone to anyone she's just met like that before."

"But Mr. Mead, we haven't just met," Monica said quickly. "I've been feeding her all the time you've been gone." The moment the words were out of her mouth, Monica regretted them. Slowly, she told herself, let him learn things slowly. What she had just done was give him another shove into that uncomfortable place Laurita called limbo.

There was a questioning look on El Pintor's face as he said, "Gone? I haven't been gone, little Monica. I've been right here waiting patiently for you and your father to arrive. And I've been preparing a welcome gift for you. Not a tuna sandwich, but something I'm more able to do than cook." He straightened in the chair and started to brush his hair back from where it had fallen across his forehead, but when his hand touched the bandage on the side of his head, he stopped. "Oho," he said, "what have we here? I must have hurt myself."

"You did," Monica said quietly and once again looked to Laurita for a signal.

"While gardening?" El Pintor asked. "I don't remember that."

"No, Señor, not while gardening," Laurita answered. "You injured your head many days ago. But maybe Monica can tell you more about that."

Monica moved restlessly in her chair, and Sopa whined a little meow of complaint. Laurita's signal was loud and clear, but Monica was afraid. What if telling him was the wrong thing to do? For a moment she held her breath, and her heart hammered loudly above Sopa's purring. Dad, she shouted silently, Dad, where are you? What am I doing here in this strange place with these strange people? Her impulse was to jump up from the chair, race out of the studio, and run, run, run. Instead, she closed her eyes and breathed deeply. What would her father tell her to do? "Always look at the facts, Monica," she could hear him saying. "They're a good basis for figuring things out." And right now El Pintor needed facts to help him. She opened her eyes and said, "I'll do my best, Mr. Mead, but I wish Rob was here to tell you what happened. It was because he was so worried about you that we found you."

El Pintor stiffened. "Found me? What's all this? I haven't been anywhere."

"Yes, you have, Señor," Laurita said decisively. "You were gone for ten days, and no one knew where you were. The entire barrio was worried about you. If it hadn't been for Roberto and this young lady, we'd still be worrying."

"But how could that be? I—"

"You've had amnesia," Monica interrupted. "That's how. You got a bump on your head and a concussion, and you forgot who you were." She bit her lip. There. She'd done it. Please, please, please don't let it hurt him.

"That's right," Laurita said softly. "You didn't know who you were. Until today. Something happened while we were gardening. It was as if your mind had made a new connection, or had healed a connection."

"Something happened, yes," El Pintor said, nodding. He touched the bandage on his head gingerly. "I was suddenly exceedingly tired. I had to get away to rest. And then I had these troubling dreams." He leaned forward and, with that apologetic little grin that Monica was becoming used to, said, "Well, young lady, and where was I for those ten days?"

"Oh, Mr. Mead," Monica said sadly, "you haven't forgotten the Callahans, have you?"

"I hope not," El Pintor said quickly. "Who are they?"

"They're the people you stayed with," Monica said. "They are really very nice and they'd be sad to think . . . well, that doesn't matter now. Anyway, I'd better start at the beginning. And I guess that was when you were at St. Francis Park nine or ten days ago. For some reason that I don't understand, you were in my old neighborhood doing some drawings. That's where St. Francis Park is, and that's where you were." Monica paused. El Pintor was listening intently, and Laurita, her dark eyes serious and sympathetic, was nodding encouragement. Monica swallowed her hesitation and with great care detailed the events that had occurred as she knew them. She told him, too, about the white painter's cap the Callahans had purchased for him and how, lacking a name, the children had called him Mr. Good Man.

During her story El Pintor interrupted only once to ask if he'd been hospitalized. When she said, "No only the emergency room," he said, "I see," and she continued. "And when Mrs. Callahan and I got home with you," she finished, "all the neighbors were waiting to see you. Like Laurita says, they'd all been really worried about you."

He nodded, but Monica sensed that he was no longer listening. He was lost in his own thoughts. The sunlight that came through the window behind his chair glistened on his white hair as he rested his head on the cushion once more. But he said nothing. Except for Sopa's rhythmic purring, the mechanical whir of the refrigerator, and, in the distance, the cries of children at play, there was silence. El Pintor's silence was not what Monica wanted. She wanted a reaction from him. She started to speak, but fear held her back. She wanted to know what he was thinking, yes. But she also wanted reassurance. She wanted to hear that nothing she'd told him was new, that except for the visit to the hospital, he'd remembered everything about the time he'd been gone. When he finally spoke, he neither calmed her fear nor reassured her.

"Those children you spoke of," he said, "are the little ones blonds and the older two redheads?"

"Yes, yes," Monica said eagerly.

El Pintor's hands were resting on his knees. He glanced down at them and then up at Monica. "But I really didn't need to ask that," he said with a smile. "Do you know what you've done? You've just recounted my troublesome dreams to me, detail by detail. Except, my dear, for one item. In my dreams it was Cristina who found me—then, suddenly, she disappeared. And no matter how I reached for her, she wasn't there."

Monica stared at him, puzzled. According to Laurita, Cristina had been his special friend, but from all she had heard, so was Rob and so was César. And it was they who had found him. Why couldn't El Pintor have reached for them?

Laurita bent over to El Pintor and patted his hand. "Dreams can be unkind, Señor Mead. Yes, Cristina is gone. I miss her, too. But I know there are others you love."

"And there are people who love you," Monica said. "All I've heard since I came here is, 'El Pintor did this,' or 'El Pintor did that.' And all the 'thises' and 'thats' were positive."

El Pintor slapped his hand on his thigh and stood up. "You're right," he said, "both of you. It's time I stopped acting like an invalid. I may have taken a blow on the head, but it was for a good cause and . . ." He stopped, wrinkled his forehead in a thoughtful frown, and turned to Monica. "The little one," he said, "her name is Annie, isn't it?"

"Yes, Mr. Mead!" Monica said joyfully. She jumped up from her chair, flinging an indignant Sopa to the floor. "Annie is the little one. You're remembering more and more. Isn't that great?"

"I think so," El Pintor said, looking around the room as if embracing it. "Yes. This room. This is where I live. These are my old worn-out books. This is my favorite chair. In that corner is my creaky bed with its scratchy Indian blanket. And over there on the counter is a sack with a sandwich you two brought me."

Laurita gave a little laugh. "Which you want to eat," she said. "And the sack's bulging. I don't know what else Monica packed for you."

"Only some chips, a banana, a candy bar, and some cookies. If that's not enough, Mr. Mead, just knock on our door." El Pintor grinned and said thank you, and the two women said goodbye. "We'll go out the back way," Monica said. As they stepped outside, she turned to wave and caught a glimpse of El Pintor settling himself back in his chair, the sandwich in his hand.

"Laurita, Laurita," she said happily as they climbed their back steps, "he's remembering."

"*No hay mal que por bien no venga,*" Laurita said somberly.

"And what does that mean?" Monica said. "Oh, no, oh, no," she added hurriedly, "I know what it means. Rosa said that all the time. It's the same as 'There's no ill wind but blows somebody good.' But what ill winds are you talking about?"

"The heavy gardening, the hot sun, your exploding at Licha. They jostled El Pintor's memory in some way. And I guess that's good."

They stepped inside the house. Monica said, "You sound worried. Did we do something wrong?"

"No, Monica, I think we did the right thing, and I'm very happy. His memory is coming back. But we have to be patient now. He's going to need time to fit those lost ten days into his life."

Monica, thinking of the letter hidden under her bed, held back a little groan. Still, if that letter had survived for all those years stuffed in a coffee can up in the attic, another week or two under the bed wouldn't cause it to disintegrate. Nor would another week or two of waiting destroy her. But patience had a pinch to it.

"I guess you're right," she said, and wondered how much patience she would need to help her through the days as they dragged by.

Chapter Seventeen

The days that followed were not what Monica had expected. They were quiet days, but they did not drag. And they were spiced with the small pleasant discoveries that new friendships always seem to provide.

Late that first afternoon, she walked up to the house with the potted marigolds to tell Toni the good news about El Pintor. Inside the house, the shades were drawn to darken the rooms. Señora Almayo had another of her migraine headaches. When Monica learned that Toni was going to walk to the drugstore to pick up her mother's pain pills, she offered to drive her. On the way back they were so busy discussing the morning's happenings that they almost missed the fact that Rob's blue pickup had been following them closely for some time.

When they pulled up at the curb in front of Monica's house, Rob's pickup gently nuzzled up against the BMW's bumper. He jumped out of the cab and ran around the back toward where the two girls stood on the sidewalk.

"Hey, you two," he called, his eyes mainly on Monica, "what's up?"

"Not much," Monica said with a straight face, "unless you call El Pintor's getting back his memory something."

Rob whooped, took her hands, spun her around a couple of times, then held her out at arm's length and shouted, "Tell me!"

So, with Toni nodding eagerly beside her, Monica repeated once more the story of all that had happened that day. Rob's face glowed. "Cool, cool," he kept saying as she talked. And when she finished he said, "As soon as I'm out of these paint-spattered clothes and have some dinner, I'll be down to see him."

Monica watched Toni scramble into the cab of the pick-up along with Rob and then she went inside to find Laurita.

That evening when Rob left the studio, he knocked on Monica's door. "I hoped you'd come over," she said. "How'd it go?"

"Good," Rob answered. "Better than good. I tried not to push him into remembering. But he came up with some memories on his own, like when we decided to paint his front door purple. He's going to be fine." He jiggled the screen door. "All right if I hang out for a while?"

"Sure," Monica said, trying to sound casual. "Let's go outside."

They sat on the porch chairs. It was really nice, Monica thought, sitting here with Rob. The day had been hot, but the evening air was cool, and the sounds of the street—the singing, the laughter, and the clang of dishes being washed—were not loud. It was nice, too, to share the joy they both felt about El Pintor.

The following day, Tuesday, all the Callahans, except for Katy and Mr. Callahan, paid a surprise visit to El Pintor. When Monica saw them, she wondered if El Pintor would have trouble placing them in the right time frame. If he did have trouble, he didn't show it. The only one who had difficulty of any kind was Annie. She had trouble saying 'Mr. Mead,' and half of the time called El Pintor 'Mr. Goodmead.'

Mrs. Callahan bubbled with pleasure at El Pintor's progress. But she was still concerned about the injury to his head. She asked several times about headaches and was finally reassured by El Pintor that they had disappeared. After that she walked enthusiastically around the studio, gazing at everything with bright eyes, filling the air with the light flower scent of her perfume.

While the two little girls entertained themselves with crayons and sketch paper, Mrs. Callahan and her serious redheaded son examined El Pintor's paintings. "I think some of these are remarkable," Mrs. Callahan said as they were leaving, "but, of course, I'm no expert." It was clear that El Pintor was pleased at her comments; it was also clear that he was very tired when the troop of Callahans finally said their goodbyes.

"We'll be back soon," Mrs. Callahan called over her shoulder as she herded the kids into the car.

"Real soon," Annie shouted. "Maybe even tomorrow."

Just after supper that evening, Monica's father came home. A yellow cab made a U-turn by their house and came to an abrupt stop at the curb by the studio. In two houses across the street, faces appeared at the doors and windows, staring openly to see who would emerge from the taxi.

Monica heard the cab and raced to the door. Her father, looking handsome and sharp in a light gray suit and her favorite gray tie, was just stepping out of the taxi. "Dad!" she cried as she flew down the steps to the sidewalk. "Dad, you're back!"

"So I am." He grinned at her, paid the driver, and turned back to give her a big hug. "Well, you look great," he said as he let her go. "How are you?"

"I'm fine, I'm fine. But, oh, how I've missed you. I have so much to tell you."

"And I you," he replied, picking up his suitcases. "But let's wait till I eat something. I had to give up supper to make this flight."

Monica couldn't wait. While he ate the bacon and eggs that Laurita and she prepared for him, she sat across the kitchen table from him, and told him of her part in the search for El Pintor, of their finding him, and how, finally, his memory had begun to return.

Her dad nodded seriously as she spoke, and when she was finished, he said, "That was good deductive thinking, Monica. Pinpointing the timing of those sketches was important. Well, I'll have to go over and see the old man before I leave."

"Leave?" Monica asked, sitting upright.

Her dad sighed. "Yes. Tomorrow night." He looked at Laurita and she nodded.

"I'll be glad to stay a few more days," she said, "unless Monica objects."

"Me object? Not on your life. If Dad has to go, you have to stay—if you will."

"I will," Laurita said. "But not tonight. I have some things to take care of at home."

When Laurita left the kitchen, Monica's father reached across the table and squeezed his daughter's hand. "I'm here because I miss you, honey, and because I needed to touch base with you and, very frankly, to pick up some more clothes."

"I see," Monica said crisply. Then in a pleading tone she added, "Dad, can't you stay another day or two?"

"Unfortunately, no. But the next time I return, which should be in a week or so, I'll be here pretty much for good. At any rate, L.A. will be my base of operations."

She had been bursting to tell him about the letter from the attic, to ask if she should open it before she showed it to El Pintor, but now she changed her mind. Her father was too involved in his own affairs to concentrate on hers. Sure, she was used to that. That had certainly been the case in Washington. But, as miserable as leaving there had been, there had been one bright side to it: she would get to spend more time with her dad. And where was that bright side now?

When her father spoke, she decided that he must have read her mind because he said, "Relax, honey. As soon as I've established the branch office down here, we'll have some—what do the social workers call it?—quality time together."

From some hidden place in her mind or heart came the thought: I'm behaving like a brat. He's struggling to make a living for us, to get out from under the unfair blow that was dealt him, and here I am adding to his load. She swallowed hard and said, "This *is* quality time. Go for it, Dad! Show them a thing or two in San Francisco!"

He gave her a long, serious look from across the table and said a quiet "Thank you."

Except for a couple of hours that he was gone on business, Monica and her dad spent all of the next day together. In between his sorting through clothes and papers, they caught up with one another. He told her of the bone-chilling fogs that roll into San Francisco nearly every afternoon and of the interesting people he had met, including the Nicaraguan chambermaid at the hotel with whom he enjoyed speaking Spanish. She told him about seeing "Springtime" and about César's stowing away on the trip to Parkview Place. Two or three times she started to tell him about the letter she had found, but each time a conviction that El Pintor should see it first stopped her. That conviction grew stronger when her father returned from visiting with El Pintor.

"We had a good long talk," he said. "He's fine. His memory is sharp and clear. He certainly was able to place me, although we've been in touch only through letters for the last few years." Her father paused for a moment, then went on. "He's only lost small fragments of time, such as the trip to the hospital and the first day or two with the Callahans. When I arrived, he was cleaning his brushes and collecting his tubes of paint. I think he's his old self again."

Later in the day she watched her dad pack his large suitcase. Then, after a supper of chicken and rice that she helped Laurita to prepare, he was gone.

The next day, Thursday, her father's visit might have been an illusion, or a minor interruption in the pattern of Monica's days. Her first thoughts on awakening each day were either for El Pintor or Rob, and in both cases, her reflections held a feeling of expectancy. With El Pintor her thought was, is this the day for the letter, and each time she decided, no, why take a chance on his not remembering it? Also, she wanted to ask why he'd been sketching around Parkview Place, but that, too, she decided, would have to wait. With Rob, her thoughts were unpredictable, sometimes thinking of their first date, sometimes annoyed at herself for falling for him. After all, what did she really know about him? Finally, she would get up, and, no matter what her earlier thoughts had been, her day was always brightened by the thought that she would see Rob that night.

Monica and Laurita checked on El Pintor a couple of times a day, trying not to interrupt him, for he had indeed returned to painting. He was working on the already started canvas that Monica had seen on the easel earlier. She wasn't certain where the grays and blues of that canvas were heading, but there was a sureness to the lines that told her that El Pintor knew, and she wondered if he was working from memory. Once in a while on their visits, she found El Pintor's eyes on her, studying her. His gaze was not disconcerting; it was too gentle. But she did wonder why. They weren't the only ones who checked on El Pintor. César came by each day, alone or with one of his ball-playing buddies. Señora Almayo came too, once carrying a large pot that Monica guessed was soup, and she was glad for Sopa's sake.

One day she and Toni went to nearby Marina del Rey and watched the sailboats and the ducks go by while they ate frozen yogurt on cones. On another, they went to an afternoon movie. It was strange being friends with the sister of a boy you dated. Kind of different. Still, everything on Lucia was different, so why not that?

For instance, there was Licha. She came to Monica's house both on Wednesday and on Friday to see how the flowers they had planted on Monday were doing. That alone seemed unusual, but on Friday she threw curious glances at the studio. Finally, she asked, "Is the old man still around? How is he?" Both Monica and Laurita stared at her in surprise.

As Licha was leaving, an ancient red sports car, its canvas top missing, squealed to a stop in the center of the street, and Josie rose up in the passenger seat. "Licha!" she yelled. "Licha, come here!"

Licha mumbled something, scrunched her shoulders, and tucked her head between them as if hiding, and kept on walking.

Josie muttered a word or two to the scraggly-haired fellow at the steering wheel and then shouted, "Screw you, Licha! You're chicken shit from now on!" She threw a fiery look at Monica and shouted, "That goes for you! I'm not through with you, remember!" Then, with a screech from its resisting tires, the red car made a sharp U-turn and raced down Lucia, sending an unwary black cat flying into the uppermost branches of the nearest pepper tree.

"I don't think she likes me," Monica said to Laurita with a grin.

"Not that," Laurita said seriously. "That girl's problem is that she doesn't like herself."

Monica shrugged. Maybe Laurita was right, but Josie certainly didn't show it. "Come on," she said. "Let's see what we can scare up for dinner."

Laurita nodded, then bent over and pinched a dry twig from a geranium slip, and together, they went into the house.

The days slipped by and it was Sunday once more. With everyone gone, including Toni and Laurita, to church and later to family doings, and Rob working on a hurry-up painting job, Sunday promised to be dull and uneventful for Monica.

Around mid-morning she went outside to water the little plants that so hopefully they had set in the soil. She was heartened by the fact that a couple of the impatiens were no longer drooping. But, no matter what Laurita claimed for them, the geranium slips, as far as she was concerned, were just dried-up sticks. When El Pintor tapped on his kitchen window, she started as if guilty of something, then caught herself and grinned and waved to him. It was strange, she told herself, to be comforted by the thought that El Pintor, at least, was close by.

That comfort was short-lived. An hour or so later she was sitting on one end of the living room couch reading when in a corner of her eye she caught sight of something white flitting by outside the house. A closer look showed her that it was El Pintor with a white painter's cap on his head and a sketch pad under his arm and that he was heading up Lucia in the direction of Chimney Hill.

She returned to the couch and picked up her book. She read a couple of paragraphs, read them again, then put the book down and went outside. There she stood on the sidewalk and watched El Pintor trudge to the end of the cracked cement sidewalk and then up the slope of Chimney Hill.

It was at that moment that she realized she had already made a decision. Her decision had been waiting for something to catapult it into awareness. And that was just what

El Pintor's white cap and his trek up to Chimney Hill had done. Yes. Her mind was made up. Absolutely. Today was the day to ask El Pintor about the letter.

Back in the house Monica flattened herself on her stomach, reached under her bed, and dragged out the old coffee can. Her breath gave a little quiver of excitement as she removed the rusty lid. Gently, she drew out El Pintor's yellowed envelope, then placed it in another envelope and sealed a bit of the flap. She knew she was being fussy, but she didn't want to take a chance on the old letter, which was already torn, tearing some more. Carefully, she slipped the envelope into the back pocket of her jeans, locked the house, and started up the street.

Chapter Eighteen

The mid-morning sun was warm as Monica started off toward Chimney Hill. The air was clear, almost crystal clear, and windless, with a canopy of bright blue sky. During the night there had been scattered thundershowers in the mountains, and the Los Angeles basin was reaping the reward of a jewel-like day.

Monica had begun walking briskly, but slowed down as she neared the hill. She still hadn't figured out how to bring up the subject. Her mind was trapped in a tangle of ideas, none of which seemed right. She sighed, a long, exasperated sigh. "Up front," she muttered as she started climbing the incline, "you've got to be up front."

The other two times she had climbed up this hill, her mind had been on other things, and she hadn't noticed how steep it was. But today, as she reached one of the ivy-covered pillars, she realized that the hill was high enough to command a narrow view of Santa Monica Bay and the mountains that surrounded it. There were a few sailboats on the water that from this distance looked like toys, and the ravines in the mountains were clear and distinct. No wonder someone had built a house up here. This spot was ideal.

Although it would soon be July, the leaves on the trees still held some of their springtime green. She envisioned the house as it must have stood by those trees. Yes, the windows on the west would have been shaded from the sun. Maybe there would have been a rose garden on the south side, and perhaps a swing had hung from the tall elm in the back. She looked sadly at the fragmented chimneys, thinking that even if this was Southern California, in a neighborhood as close as this to the ocean, a fireplace burning cheerily was probably very welcome at times. She thought of the woman in El Pintor's painting. Had she been the owner of this house? If so, had she come from some cold climate where so many chimneys would not have been unusual? Who was she? And what had El Pintor to do with her? And, for that matter, where was El Pintor?

Above her she heard the rustling of wings as two small brown birds exploded from a nearby elm, announcing the arrival of several crows that, with a chorus of demanding "caws," settled on the elm's uppermost branches. Where was El Pintor? Monica picked her way carefully on the weed-grown gravel drive, past what must have been the front entry, and along the crumbling cement wall that was all that was left of the foundation on the west side. Scraggly, overgrown shrubs grew by the cement foundation and intertwined with those beneath the trees, making it difficult to get by them. The only shrub she recognized and could name was plumbago, the one with the blue flowers, and that only because it so often grew beside the freeways.

Finally, she went past the last of the sprawling bushes, pushing back an obstinate branch, and found herself in a narrow clearing bounded directly in front of her by a tall, thick hedge.

She looked to each side of her. On her right, beyond several dry, dead shrubs, lay the disintegrating stack of one of the chimneys. On her left, she could see the gradual slope of the scrub-laden hillside. El Pintor, if he was still on this hill, had to be on the other side of the hedge. And there was no way around it. The hedge's ragged limbs intertwined with the dry bushes and the scrub growth on each side, producing an impenetrable tangle. But in its center there was an area of bent and broken branches, as if someone had pushed through it. At least, she thought, she could see what was on the other side. At eye level the hedge was too thickly grown, so she parted the branches at waist level and bent over to peer through them.

On the other side of the hedge, seated in the shelter of a six-sided little summerhouse, was El Pintor. It was a small wooden building, with a peaked roof covered with bird droppings and leaves. Closer to the hedge through which she was looking there seemed to be a little path beaten into the ground. It was clear that she had come the wrong way. The path obviously started on the other side of the hill. As she watched, El Pintor held up his sketch book, looking at it critically. She thought of calling out to him, and was debating whether or not to do so, when she felt something tug at the back of her jeans.

She spun around. Josie stood on the other side of the narrow clearing. A long, black T-shirt hung loosely from her small, bony shoulders, with only a whisper of red shorts showing below the bottom of the shirt. The green stripe in Josie's red hair had faded, and on the top of her head a remarkable circle of black hair roots was showing. Monica noticed these things, but what really held her eyes was the white envelope in Josie's hand.

"Where'd you get that?" she said. Her hand went to the back pocket of her jeans and found it empty. "You took it!" she cried. "Give it back!"

"Get real," Josie said with a laugh. "Whatever this is, it's mine now. It's in the program. I owe you one."

Something leaden, maybe her heart, sank to Monica's stomach. Her shoulders sagged as she thought, this isn't happening. She felt hot tears welling up behind her eyes and blinked them back furiously. Suddenly, anger at Josie, at her feelings of helplessness, surged up in her. It was at that moment that Josie decided to look down at the envelope. Monica shot like a rocket across the few feet that separated them. With a quick down thrust of her arm she sent the white envelope flying from Josie's hands. It slid under the tangled shrubbery, and Monica dove for it. So did Josie.

They both ended up flat on their stomachs by the low-growing bushes, each squirming to reach the white rectangle. Josie, muttering obscenities, snaked past Monica and, with more curses as brambles scraped her arms, gave one more push and her fingers touched the envelope.

"No, you don't!" Monica muttered, trying desperately to stretch as far as Josie had. It was no use. Josie had found the only spot in the jumble of branches that allowed an arm and a shoulder through. Monica was left a foot behind her. She tried pushing Josie to one side, and when she did, Josie's left hand curled into a fist and gave her a vicious jab in the ribs.

"Aow-w-w-w!" Monica groaned. All in one movement she pushed up on her left elbow, grabbed a thick handful of Josie's sticky hair with her right hand, and pulled.

Josie shrieked. Through clenched teeth she cried, "Don't do that!" And then she lay absolutely still.

Monica had expected any number of things from Josie: kicks, shoves, even bites, but not this. Why wasn't she fighting back? The answer came almost immediately. Josie started once more to hit Monica, but stopped, gasping, when Monica tightened the pull on her hair. So that was it! Josie was one of those people whose scalp was so sensitive that even brushing could cause unbearable pain.

Monica exhaled. All's fair in love and war, and this was a war that Josie had started. "Take your hands off my letter," she threatened, "or I'll pull your hair out, all of it!" She tightened her hold on Josie's hair.

This time Josie screamed, a muffled scream since her hands were clawing the earth and her face was pressed against them. "Let go!" she cried. "Let go! You can have your old letter."

"I'll let go when you slide away from it," Monica said, releasing some of the pressure. "But if I slide back and you don't, your hair is really going to get pulled. Here I go."

Slowly, the two girls inched away from the bushes, Monica still holding a handful of Josie's hair.

"Let go now," Josie muttered when they were lying in the center of the clearing. "I'm not gonna hassle you. I gotta take care of my head. You've gone and done it. It'll never heal now."

"Heal?" Monica said. "Come on, it wasn't that bad." She moved away from Josie and scanned the clearing. Not two feet away from her she saw a length of deadwood the width of her arm. She reached for it, and as she did, she let go of Josie's hair. Josie pushed herself upright. Monica gripped the bough, ready to use it. But there was no need.

Josie was as limp and worn as a discarded rag doll. And she was crying. "It'll never heal now," she moaned through tears that made rivulets on her dusty face. "That rotten dye burned my scalp and it was healing, but you've gone and ruined it all. The skin's probably all broken again."

"Maybe you asked for it," Monica said quietly. What she wished she could say was, "I'm sorry. Oh, I'm sorry if I hurt you." But she knew that wasn't possible.

Josie shot a look at Monica that dripped with venom and spit on the ground near her. Then, pulling apart the shrubs behind her, she ducked through them and stalked away.

Monica listened to the crunching sounds of Josie's footsteps until she could hear them no more. Then, using the bough in her hand, she dragged the envelope from beneath the bush. She dusted it, dusted herself, and started the long way around to the summerhouse. By the time she found the little path on the other side of the ruins, she had calmed down. The scuffle with Josie had left her shaking, but, at last, her hands were steady, and her heart and breath were both behaving. It was all right. Now she could talk to El Pintor.

The path on the east side of the ruins, although well-worn, was dusty, and here and there was crossed by a low-growing plant with dark green leaves and fragile purple flowers. When she stepped on one of its tendrils, she smelled a familiar musky scent. Lantana. On Parkview it had climbed all over the service yard wall. The path led her under the elm tree and along the remains of a low picket fence that was barely visible under a cover of the purple-flowered lantana. Its scent was stronger here, pungent, dusty. It was clear that this hill had long ago been abandoned. And yet, she thought, this trail must be used regularly or it wouldn't exist; it would be overgrown. Now the path took a sudden turn around a huge oleander shrub, and she was facing the summerhouse. Monica paused, examining it.

What she hadn't been able to see through the hedge was that the summerhouse was built on a high wooden base, with six wide stairs leading to its entry.

She pulled the envelope from her pocket and took another couple of steps. "Mr. Mead," she called softly. "Mr. Mead, it's Monica." When there was no answer, she walked to the bottom of the steps and looked up to the entry. "Mr. Mead, it's Monica," she said more firmly. "May I come talk to you?"

There was a movement above her in the summerhouse, and El Pintor appeared at the top of the stairs. "Why, Monica," he said. "Hello. Come on up. I was just thinking of you."

"It's E.S.P.," she said with a grin. The steps, she noticed as she started up them, were solid and firm, with not even a squeak as she put her weight on them. Although the summerhouse was desperately in need of paint—its once white pillars and ceiling were now a murky gray with only a few stubborn flakes of paint clinging to them—she could see that repairs had been made to the railing and the bench that ran alongside it.

As she stepped into the summerhouse, she said, "I know I'm interrupting what you're doing, drawing or meditating or whatever, but I have something important to ask you."

"I need to be interrupted," he said. "Sometimes I sit too long, just looking at the ocean and dreaming. It's not good for old men to dream too much. Here, let's sit here." He

indicated the bench where his sketch pad and white painter's cap lay.

They sat facing a small view of the rooftops of Venice and South Santa Monica and, beyond them, the ocean. Monica swallowed hard, cleared her throat, and, holding out the envelope, said, "This letter belongs to you, Mr. Mead. Or rather, to my mother. But you wrote it a long time ago."

"What's this?" El Pintor's blue eyes widened as he turned to look at her. "A letter? A letter I wrote to your mother? I don't remember that at all."

Monica tore open the covering white envelope. "Maybe if you read it, you'd remember." Carefully, she drew out the old yellowed envelope. "See? You even signed it."

He took it from Monica and held it lightly in his hands. It seemed to her that he was staring at the envelope blankly, but his next remark showed that she was wrong.

"Yes," he said, nodding, his eyes still on the letter, "yes, I wrote this many years ago. And I also remember what prompted me to do so." He turned the envelope over. "It's still sealed. Of course. She died before she could read it." He raised his head and looked out into the distance. Monica said nothing. She didn't know what to say. Finally, El Pintor turned to her. "Did your father have this?" he asked.

"Oh, no," she said quickly. "He would have returned it to you if he had. My mother had it. I mean, she put it away in a special place. To open it later, like you said, when her parents died. But when she got married, I think she forgot to take it with her, because it was still in this house." She went on to tell him about her mother's secret hiding place and how she had found it. "But I didn't want to read it," she finished, "without first asking your permission."

She took a deep breath, and the frustrations of the last couple of weeks spilled out in words. "It was hard not to, though, since you were gone and nobody knew where you were or if you'd be coming back. And then when we found you, your memory was gone, and I thought it might never come back and what was the use of waiting, but it looked to me like it was an important letter to you, so I did wait."

He smiled at her. "It is important to me. I'm glad you waited. You were very patient."

"Laurita kept telling me to be patient," she said. "Not about the letter—I haven't told anyone about it—but about your memory. I mean, when it would come back."

"So it's our secret," he said. "Maybe it would be best if I kept it just my secret."

"Oh, no," she said, her voice heavy with disappointment. "You mean you're not going to let me read it?"

He took a deep breath, and his eyes circled the hill, pausing at the ruins of the house and finally returning to look out at the ocean. He breathed out, a great, gusty sigh. "No, my dear," he said, "you shall read it. It's the right thing to do." His large hand patted hers, and he handed her the letter.

"Now?" she asked.

"Yes. It's as good a time as any, and as good a place." He got up, crossed to the other side of the summerhouse, and, with his back to her, stood looking at the view.

Monica stared at the writing on the envelope. ". . . to be opened on the death of her parents." And below that in her mother's hand, "I promised El Pintor. I won't even tell Laurita . . ." Monica nodded. Yes. Waiting for El Pintor had been the right thing to do. She turned the sealed envelope over, and as she did, the yellowed paper fell apart here and there, wisps of it floating in the air, then tumbling down to the floor like little dry leaves. The letter itself was in better condition than its covering.

Tremulously, she unfolded it. "My dearest Cristina," it started. She glanced up at El Pintor. His back was still turned to her.

I do not write this lightly. It took days of debating about whether or not to tell you what you are about to learn before I arrived at a conclusion. This letter is the result. We are old friends, so you know that I am a man with many faults, and perhaps that will explain some of my actions.

She looked up as she heard a shout from the path below them. Three glistening black crows flew noisily from the roof of the summerhouse as César shot up the steps to the entry. "El Pintor!" he yelled. "I came for you! Those people are at your house. The ones you lived with. And they've got a man who wants to see you. I told them I'd get you because I knew where you were. And here I am!"

Chapter Nineteen

Monica sat alone in the summerhouse, the sheets of El Pintor's letter lying loosely on her lap. It was more than thirty minutes since she had watched El Pintor and César tramp down the steps and around the tall olean-der shrub, César chattering excitedly as they went. It was five minutes since she had finished reading the letter Cristina for the third time, and she was still trying to absorb what it meant.

She looked over her shoulder at the broken chimneys and shuddered. So this had been El Pintor's house and that of the lovely lady in the painting as well. And a baby girl, a two-month-old baby girl, had lived here, too. Until the night of the fire. She picked up the papers on her lap and read once more:

> The fire was purely accidental. A spark from the fireplace, a flammable cushion nearby on the floor while Sara and the baby were asleep upstairs, and I out with some friends. When I got home, the fire was almost controlled and Sara was dead. She had been able to toss the baby from a second-story window to

the waiting firemen below, but it was too late for her; she was trapped.

I won't try to describe what happened to me. I probably couldn't anyway. All I remember is the nightmare experience of the next few days. Luckily, the baby was in good hands. Your mother, Chita, who had been with Sara since her return from the maternity hospital, took the child at the scene of the fire, and later that night took me in, too.

Monica stopped reading, closed her eyes, and sighed. She didn't want to read again what came next. Finally, she opened her eyes, picked up the sheet she had dropped, and read on:

I'm not proud of what happened next. Yes, I did the things I was supposed to do. I buried my sweet Sara. I took care of what had to be done in regard to the ruins of the house on the hill. Then, after that was done, one dark night when the blackness over-whelmed me, I left a note for Chita and Ramón Salas, and, without even a kiss for my darling child, I ran.

No need to tell you how far I ran, or how I ran. All you need to know is how long I was gone. Well over a year. And then one day I wanted to see my child. Was she walking? Was she talking? Whom was she calling Daddy? I had to know. So I returned. Sur-prisingly, Ramón and Chita were glad to see me and made me welcome in their home. They are two of the kindest people in the world.

I arrived early one morning while their little family was at breakfast. It was obvious that they were a family and that I was an outsider. My child was beautiful and unafraid. She allowed me to hold her. But when I spoke to her, calling her Daphne, she pulled away from me and ran to Chita. "Her name is Cristina," Ramón explained, and I realized that they had made her their child. What could I expect? I had abandoned her to wallow in my grief. And once I was tired of coddling that grief, I had allowed her into my thoughts and then returned to claim her, as if she was an item I had placed in storage.

In the days that followed, my awareness grew of the love that overspread that household. I learned, too, that the people now living on Lucia accepted that Daphne was Cristina and the daughter of Chita and Ramón. Few had known my wife and me before the fire; none knew me now. As the time grew near for me to leave, I struggled with the thought of the pain I would inflict on these good people when I took Cristina—by now she was Cristina—away. There were other considerations. Except for the property on the hill, I was penniless. After Sara's death, I had squandered and gambled away all that I had. My paintings had gone in the fire. Only two that had been at the framer's on that night remained, and those I would not sell.

It shows you what state of mind I was in, how bleakly I surveyed the future, when I tell you that when Ramón and Chita made a proposition to me, I accepted hungrily. I persuaded myself that you needed a mother, but I know the decision served me, too. And, in truth, I do not regret it. I believe you have had a better life for it. They adopted you. Legally. We made one another a promise to keep your true identity our secret—a promise that until now we have kept. I was to be allowed a home beside them until I was once more on my feet. Those blessed people had adopted me, too.

The first few years were difficult; there were adjustments to be made on both sides. But it was your acceptance and love of your parents that made it all real. You were their child; I was your special friend. You know the rest, Cristina. Over the years we built the studio, and I found a sense of peace and a purpose in life.

Perhaps, it is another weakness of character that has allowed me to write this letter. I feel a great need to confess, and by confessing to blot out the crime, I committed when I abandoned you. After that deplorable action and that degrading period of my life, I have made it a point always to be here for you. I hope you will keep that in mind as you think over what you have learned here.

Your friend and father,
Francis Mead

Monica drew in a great breath and let it out slowly. Hot tears spilled onto her cheeks as she threw the papers on the floor. How dare he? How dare he have written this letter? How could he expect my mother to forgive him? She jumped up and went to stand where El Pintor had stood, his back to her. She stared across the rooftops to the sky and to its reflection in the glistening ocean below it. She was glad that César had come for El Pintor. She couldn't have faced him. Well, she *could* have, but she didn't want to. In a moment she turned, scooped up the pages of the letter, and sat on the bench once more. The sheets beside her drew her eyes like magnets, but she pulled them away and shook her head. No sense in reading it again. The words certainly wouldn't have changed, nor would El Pintor's lame excuses.

"Lame, lame, lame," she muttered.

"Hey, what's up? Why are you talking to yourself?" Rob, smiling, took the steps of the summerhouse two at a time. "César told me I'd find you here."

"Rob? I thought you'd be working."

"I thought so, too, but our customer changed her mind. Didn't want us around on a Sunday after all." Rob came and sat beside her. "What're you doing? Writing a letter?"

"No. Reading one. From El Pintor. It's an old letter. He wrote it to my mother and I—" She sighed, shook her head and turned away. "Oh, Rob, it's so mixed up."

He placed his hands on her shoulders and gently turned her to face him. "You've been crying," he said. "What's up, Monica?"

She thrust the letter at him. She had made no promise to keep it a secret, and even if she had . . . "Here. This will tell you."

Rob took his time reading it. Once he said "Holy Christmas" softly, shook his head, and went on reading.

Monica was too edgy to remain sitting, so she got up and walked around the summerhouse, pausing a couple of times to look out at the overgrown hillside. When he was done, Rob came to stand beside her. He smiled broadly as he handed her the letter.

"I can see why you were crying," he said. "You've found a grandfather, and, wow, he's El Pintor! You couldn't do better than that!"

Monica gave him a long look. Then she threw the letter at him. For the second time in ten minutes, El Pintor's handwritten pages scattered on the floor.

"What's that about?" Rob said as he bent over to retrieve them. "What did I do?" He straightened the pages out and abruptly burst out laughing. "You sure like to throw things, don't you?"

"Not always." Monica laughed as she sat on the bench again. "Anyway, you really didn't do anything. It was El Pintor who did." But there was no laughter in her eyes as she added, "He abandoned my mother."

"Good Lord, Monica, that was a million years ago."

"That doesn't matter. How *could* he? How could he have done that?"

"I don't know," Rob said seriously and came and sat beside her. "Like they say, I've never walked in his shoes. I don't know how I'd act if someone I loved died, burned up like that. I don't know, but I think, maybe, I'd go a little crazy, too."

Monica shrugged and spread her arms in a gesture of doubt. "You could look at it that way, I guess," she said. "But how about when he came back? Why did he do what he did then? He just gave her away. Like she was a doll or something."

Rob threw her a sharp quick look, then turned back to inspect a spot on the floor between his feet. "I don't know," he said, talking to the spot on the floor, "but maybe he had his reasons. Maybe he knew he'd be a better friend than a parent. He kind of says that in the letter. You know, Monica, I think you ought to read it again more slowly."

"I've already read it three times." Then, with a glance at Rob's troubled face, "But, all right. I'll read it again, but not right now. Later. Tonight, maybe."

She jumped up. "I'd better get back," she said to Rob, who had stood up, too. "Laurita won't have a clue as to where I am."

"Oh, yes, she will. Have you forgotten César?"

"Yes," she said with a grin, "I had. But I'd better go anyway."

"All right," Rob said, and they circled the ruins and went down the hill.

With every step she took, Monica told herself that she didn't want to see El Pintor. He would be expecting her to respond to the letter. And whatever response he was looking for—joy, gladness, surprise, or even anger—she wouldn't have it. Her feelings were a tangled mess. What she needed was time, time alone, to unravel them. She hoped that he would be inside the studio, so that she could avoid him. When Rob and she neared her house and she saw the Callahan's blue van parked beyond her dad's car, she breathed more easily.

They stopped at the walkway to her house. Monica felt Rob's hand brush hers, and she turned and smiled at him.

He took her hand and squeezed it as he said, "See you later? Maybe that movie we missed?"

"I'd like that. So long as we don't talk about this." She held up the letter. Once they agreed on the time he'd pick her up, Rob left and Monica went inside. She walked quickly into her bedroom and buried the letter under papers in her desk drawer.

"Is that you, Monica?" Laurita called. "Come into the back bedroom. See what's going on with El Pintor."

Laurita was standing at a window that overlooked the space between the garage and the studio. Monica joined her and saw three roughly framed canvases leaning against one of the open garage doors. As she looked, El Pintor and a lithe blond man wearing jeans and sneakers came out of the garage, each carrying another painting. They placed the paintings against the second garage door, and the stranger, adjusting gold-rimmed glasses on his nose, stepped back and examined them.

"Who is that man?" Monica asked. "Do you know?"

"Of course I do," Laurita said with a grin. "César keeps bringing me reports. The man's name is Ralph, so César says, and he's a good friend of the Callahans. Ralph owns a store where they sell paintings, and he really likes El Pintor's paintings so, according to César, he's probably going to sell them, too." Laurita nudged Monica. "Look at César. He's not missing a word."

César sat on his haunches by the studio door, his eyes following every move the two men made, his ears, undoubtedly, tuned to catch every word.

Laurita turned away from the window and sighed. "*No hay mal que por bien no venga,*" she said. "El Pintor's ill wind may be blowing him some good. I'm talking about his accident and his amnesia. Because he had to meet the Callahans so that they'd see his paintings and be impressed by them and bring an art expert to look at them."

Monica, thinking of what she had just learned from the letter, said, "It's strange how things happen. I guess if I'd never come here, I'd be feeling different today. I don't mean that I've had anything to do with what's going on out there—"

"But you did," Laurita interrupted. "What do you think El Pintor was doing in your old neighborhood? He was drawing a series of pictures that would have special meaning for one person. And that person was you. When he learned you were coming here to live, he started putting them together as a gift for you."

"For me? How do you know?"

"Oh, we talked. He was one of the regulars at the guitar shop. In fact—" Laurita stopped abruptly, and Monica looked at her in surprise.

"In fact what?" she said.

"Nothing important. I was just going to say that he was my father's good friend. And that the two of them were at the Sonora Café drinking and talking the night of the fire on Chimney Hill. My father never forgave himself." Laurita shrugged. "As if the fire had been his doing."

"So he was out with the guys. El Pintor wasn't much of a family man, was he?"

Laurita gave her a piercing look. "Why do you say that? Of course he was. As I heard it, the two men were celebrating something. A loan paid off, a painting sold, a beautiful guitar just finished. *¿Qué se yo?* What do I know? But enough of the past." She motioned toward the window. "If this turns out to be a good thing for El Pintor, we'll really have something to celebrate."

"I guess," Monica said, wishing for Laurita's sake that she could round up some enthusiasm. "I guess that would be nice."

Laurita turned to look at her again. "You look tired," she said. "Aren't you feeling well?"

"I'm okay. I had a run-in with Josie up on the hill. She tried pushing me around and I pushed back. Actually, I pulled her hair, not knowing that she'd ruined her scalp with some stupid dye, and she freaked out." Monica had trouble meeting Laurita's eyes as she said that; she didn't like to lie, even by omission. "Anyway, she asked for it."

"That girl is bad news," Laurita said. "You'll feel better after lunch. Come on. I picked up a pizza on the way home from church. Let's put it in the oven for a few minutes."

The pizza smelled wonderful as it came out of the oven, and Monica sat down to eat it with eagerness. But even though Laurita was obviously enjoying it, bite after bite of her own wedge proved hard to swallow. The pepperoni seemed flat and tasteless, the warm, melting cheese, rubbery and dull.

Chapter Twenty

Twelve hours later, a little after midnight, Monica sat on the edge of her bed in the sheltering darkness of her room. She kicked off her slippers and slid under the lightweight summer blanket. Lying back on her pillow, she gazed at the shadows that a lamplight across the street angled onto the ceiling and thought back happily on the evening just past.

Rob and she had gone to a movie and after that, stopped at McDonald's for cheeseburgers and fries. She had been starving because, although she had managed to avoid El Pintor all afternoon, the confusion of thoughts the letter provoked dulled her appetite both for lunch and dinner. She not only ate all of her french fries but half of Rob's, and he just grinned and offered to buy her more. Rob was—well, there was no other way to put it—Rob was sweet. It was hard to imagine that he had ever been the misguided tough guy that he claimed to have been, a member of a gang of swaggering, knife-wielding, pot-smoking twelve-year-olds. Until El Pintor got to him.

Over two refills of Pepsi, Rob told her how El Pintor had weaned him away from his gang. He had done it, he said, by giving him paying jobs, by lending him books that they discussed together, by talking about what it meant to be a painter in a serious adult way until one day he discovered that he was bored with his gangmates. "Of course, that wasn't all he did," Rob said. "He lectured me. In my face. Sometimes he came at it differently, talking about the dumb things he had done when he was young. And the one time that the cops got after me, he was there for me. Kept me from getting a record." Rob finished by saying, "Another year in that gang and I would have been dead meat."

Now in her bed Monica tried to remember what they had talked about next, but her attempt at remembering was short-lived because she fell asleep. Troubling dreams filled her sleep, so that when she was awakened abruptly, she felt relief. Someone was calling her name. She twisted around, raising her head slightly, and mumbled, "Dad? What's up?" No. Her dad was in San Francisco. She sat up and called, "Laurita? Laurita, is something wrong?" And then she smelled the smoke.

In the distance she heard a siren and then at her window, a loud pounding. "Monica! Monica!" someone shouted. "Do you hear me?"

"I hear you, I hear you," she called breathlessly and scrambled out of bed.

"Climb out the window," came the reply. "Don't go through the house. The doors are in flames." It was El Pintor, his voice growing more distant as he ran to the back of the house where he called to Laurita.

Monica pulled on her slippers, threw up the window, and began tugging at the hook that held the window screen in place. It gave and she shoved the screen outward. She had pulled one leg over the sill and was about to bring the other leg over when she thought of El Pintor's letter. She swung her feet to the floor, dug into her desk drawer, and then scrambled out the window, dropping to the ground below it with the old envelope in her hand. She hurried to the back of the house in time to see Laurita in a long cotton robe lowering herself from the window that they had stood at earlier in the day. For a moment Laurita struggled with the robe she was wearing as it caught on a rough spot on the wooden sill, but soon she was free and on the ground, too. El Pintor, fully dressed, had the garden hose in hand and was shooting a stream of water at the brilliant orange flames that engulfed the back door and the back porch railing.

Monica raced to the front of the house, heading toward the hose that was coiled by El Pintor's front door. She shoved the letter in her hand under the doormat and began to unroll the hose. As she did, two fire engines rolled to a rumbling stop in front of the studio. "Hurry!" she called to the firemen who in an instant were on the ground and at their tasks. "Hurry, please. The front door is burning!"

Forgetting for a bit the terror of the fire, Monica watched with fascination as the firefighters moved through the eerie, light-spattered darkness. It's like a pattern in a basketball game, she thought; they each know where to go and what to do. And then the surging waves of smoke that choked her and stung her eyes brought her back to the horror of the moment. Neighbors poured out of their houses, to huddle in groups of three and four at the edge of the activity. They were quickly directed to stand across the street.

In a matter of minutes the fire at both the doors was out. Two firemen inspected the interior of the house, while others examined the outside doors, and they came to two conclusions. The first was that the house was safe for habitation, that the doors were deeply scorched, but lockable. The second conclusion was that the fires were the work of an arsonist, having been started at each site with gasoline-soaked rags and papers.

Monica and Laurita were standing pressed against the studio wall watching the firemen pack their gear when they heard that the fire had been set deliberately. Laurita closed her eyes and sighed. Monica shuddered.

"Are you cold?" Laurita asked.

Monica shook her head. "If I'm shaking, it's not from cold, it's from the scare I got." She glanced down at the shortie pajamas she was wearing. "I didn't even grab a robe." With a smile she indicated the people who had gathered across the street. "I hope the neighbors aren't shocked."

Laurita patted her shoulder. "We'll be going in in a minute."

"Not yet, though. Here comes the fire chief, or whatever he's called."

A tall redheaded fireman approached them. He spoke to Laurita. "Are you the lady of the house?"

"I guess I am," Monica said. "My dad's away on business. Laurita's staying with me."

The fireman wiped sweat from his forehead with a rumpled white handkerchief and turned to Monica. "As far as you know, does your father have any enemies who would want to harm you?"

"Enemies? I don't think so."

Laurita threw her a doubting glance. "Are you forgetting Josie?" she asked.

Monica frowned. "Not really. But she's not after Dad."

"That was going to be my next question," the fireman said. "Do you have any enemies? Do you belong to a gang?"

"Me?" Monica said indignantly. How dare he ask her such a thing? Couldn't he see she wasn't a gang type? She was searching for something caustic to reply when her sense of humor took over and her indignation melted away. Rich girls, poor girls, private-school girls, and gang girls, she told herself, probably all look alike in rumpled pajamas and tangled hair. "No," she said evenly, "I don't belong to a gang. I was in a private school in Virginia until a few weeks ago."

"But for some reason this Josie had it in for you?" he asked.

"I guess so."

"Monica, Monica," Laurita said, shaking her head. "You know so. She's been out to get you since you caught her splattering paint on the houses."

The fireman turned to Monica and with a little laugh said, "Does your friend Josie have red-and-green hair?"

Monica nodded. "And black roots," she added dryly.

"Well, then," he said, "I think you can sleep soundly for what's left of the night. The police found someone answering to that description dumping gasoline-soaked rags in the trash bin behind Colwell's drugstore. And that young woman will have a lot of explaining to do. Arson is too cruel a crime to be taken lightly. Well, goodnight, ladies."

"Arson," Monica whispered to herself. Then, as she heard the motors of the fire trucks starting, she called, "Goodnight! And thank you, thank you!"

The two great fire engines roared down the street. In their wake, one of the neighbors, a plaid robe hanging loosely over her nightgown, hurried across the street toward them. She was one of the women Monica had seen sitting on her front steps, talking and laughing with a friend.

"Oh, no," Monica moaned. "She's coming over to be nosy."

Laurita shrugged. "Maybe not, maybe not. Let's wait and see."

"*Que cosa,*" the woman said, wrapping her robe tightly around her stocky body. "What a thing. Are you all right? Is there anything we can do for you?" Laurita assured her that all was fine, that the firemen had said the house was safe and that they were just going in to go to bed. The chunky woman nodded, murmuring "*Gracias a Dios,*" and, as hurriedly as she had come, returned across the street

Monica turned to Laurita with an embarrassed shrug. "When I'm wrong, I'm really wrong," she said.

"Not that wrong," Laurita answered. "Our neighbor held herself back because she saw how tired we are. The questions will come tomorrow. Look, they're all leaving now, so why don't we go in, too."

"You go ahead. There's something out here I have to get."

"I'll start opening the windows then. We'll need to air the house out for a while."

Monica, already on her way to the front of the studio, called over her shoulder, "I'll be in to help you." A few more steps brought her to the corner of the small building, and she tiptoed cautiously through the flower bed. Halfway through she stopped. Someone was huddled on the bench on the far side of the door. In the pale yellow light cast by the lamp across the street, she saw that the figure was that of El Pintor.

"Mr. Mead," she called, "Mr. Mead, are you all right?"

On the bench El Pintor raised his head slowly. "I'm all right," came the reply in a voice that was low and uncertain.

"Are you sure?"

"Sure? Yes, I'm sure."

Monica, forgetting all about the flowers, tramped through them to sit on the bench beside him. He said nothing, and she leaned back against the studio's wall, listening to the almost quiet night. Finally, she said, "The firemen are gone."

"Yes, I saw."

"The house isn't in bad shape. The doors will even lock."

"Good."

A snail struggled across a small section of a stepping stone at their feet. Monica watched its progress for a moment and then asked, "Was it you who called the firemen?"

"Yes. And the police."

"You saw Josie," she said simply.

"Yes. But not in time to stop her. I needed to get you out of the house."

Monica wanted to say, "And once we were safe, you came and hid over here to get away from the horror of another fire." She stared at him, wondering what strength of will he must have called on to do all the things that he had done. If I'm the tiniest bit like you, she thought, I guess I'll be lucky. She stood up. "I'd better go in now. Laurita will be wondering where I am." She bent over and reached for the envelope under the doormat.

"Ah-h-h," he said quietly. "You saved the letter."

"Yes. I was afraid it would burn up with the house, and I didn't want it to."

He gave her a long, appraising look. "Have you read it?"

"Yes."

"I wondered. I waited, but you never came to talk to me about it."

"No. I . . . I couldn't."

"I see." El Pintor sat back and rubbed his eyes with his fingertips. Then, nodding his head in resignation, he said, "What's done is done. And old sins cast long shadows."

"There were no sins!" she said, quickly dropping to her knees beside him. "I couldn't talk to you because I was all mixed up about that, and I'm glad I didn't. Please, believe me. I was so mixed up."

"Maybe if we'd talked, I might have answered some of your questions."

"I couldn't. I read the letter over and over again. I had to figure it out all by myself." She thought of Rob and added, "Well, almost all by myself."

He sighed, a long shuddering sigh, and she said, "Why, you're trembling. You must be cold."

"No, I'm not cold. Just tired. It's been a long day."

"I know." She squeezed his hand. "But it is cold. I think you should go in now, Grandfather."

Chapter Twenty-One

When Monica returned to her house, she found Laurita in the kitchen. She was seated at the table, staring blankly into a mug of hot milk that she held cupped with both hands. Monica hesitated at the kitchen door.

Laurita straightened up, sighed, and ran her fingers through her short black hair. "I'm glad you're back," she said. "I closed the doors to our bedrooms and opened the others. I think we'll be all right." With a quick little smile, she added, "Did you find El Pintor?"

Monica threw her a sharp look. And then, as if a spotlight had been thrown on it, she saw the truth. "You've known all along, haven't you?" she said.

"Come. Sit down. There's enough hot milk for you, too." Monica washed her hands, poured herself some milk, and sat across from her. "My father was his friend, you know," Laurita said.

"But why didn't you tell me?"

"*Ay, linda,* I wanted to, but I couldn't. *Cada cabeza es un mundo.* We each live in our own world. It was for him to tell you when he was ready."

Monica studied the curling ribbons of steam rising from her cup. "I wonder if he would have," she said. "I mean, if I hadn't found that letter." She looked across the table at Laurita and, with a little intake of breath, said, "But you don't know about the letter. It was with those other things I found in the attic. It was sealed—my mother never had a chance to read it—and she had written a note on the envelope saying that she would keep it secret, not telling anyone at all that she had it.

"After a whole lot of thinking about it, I decided that no matter how much I wanted to, I couldn't read the letter or tell anyone about it until I had talked with El Pintor."

Laurita grinned. "So that's why you were so eager to find him."

"I could hardly wait. It took all the will power I had not to read it. And to think that you knew all along what was in it."

"No, no," Laurita said quickly. "I didn't even know that letter existed. I only learned who El Pintor was after Cristina died. With Ramón Salas, your . . . well, your first grandfather in a nursing home and both your grandmother and mother dead, my parents must have felt it was safe to tell me what they knew about Cristina. But, as to the letter, I have no idea what El Pintor wrote in it."

"I'm sure it's all right for you to read it now. Would you like to?"

"Of course I would, but your father should see it first."

"Dad! Oh, Lord. With all the commotion, I forgot about Dad." Suddenly there were tears filling her eyes, and she bit her lip to keep it from trembling. "I know it's after two o'clock, Laurita, but I kind of need him. Do you think I should I call him?"

"I think he'd expect you to."

Monica hurried to the table in the hallway. Sitting on the floor with the phone on her lap, she was surprised to see that her hand was shaky as she pressed the numbers of her dad's hotel.

"Room 1210," she said and waited through four rings before she heard his crisp "Hello." Only she would have guessed that her father was still half asleep. "I'm all right, Dad. It's Monica," she said, following the pattern they'd agreed to for unexpected phone calls.

"Monica! What is it? What's going on, honey?"

The tears were threatening to spill over. She swallowed hard, held them back, and said, "Too much, Dad. I can't handle it alone."

"For god's sake *what*, honey? Tell me."

"Somebody set the house on fire. It's all right. It was just the doors, but the ugly part is that someone was out to get me; that's why it happened." Now the tears could not be held back. "I'm not really crying, Dad, really. But do you think you could come home?"

"I'll leave immediately. But are you really all right? Are you sure the house is safe?"

"Everything's okay. The firemen said so, and Laurita and I checked. And El Pintor's right next door. He was great. Oh, Dad, I have so much to tell you. Please hurry."

With the comforting promise of her father's return held close, Monica crept into bed once more and, hoping he'd be the one to awaken her, fell asleep swiftly. But it was not her father's arrival that awakened her the next morning. Through that hazy uncertainty that is neither sleep nor wakefulness, she became aware of a series of dull taps and a hushed conversation that came, she thought, from the front of the house. Once awake, she could not ignore them. She slid out of bed and, wrinkling her nose at the stinging smell of last night's fire, hurried through the living room and pulled open the outside door.

Three surprised faces looked up at her. El Pintor and Rob were hunched over the sill, obviously thrown off balance by the sudden opening of the door. Laurita, sitting on the porch rail, a cup of coffee in her hand, muffled a laugh as she spoke.

"Monica, I'm sorry. It's not their fault. I convinced them you'd sleep through anything. And they weren't making that much noise. What woke you up?"

"I don't know. I think they did. What're you two doing, anyway?" This last to the two men on the porch floor.

El Pintor answered. "We were checking out the doors. We'll see what your father has to say about them, but both Rob and I think they ought to be replaced."

Rob, dressed in the usual khaki shorts and white T-shirt, grinned up at her. His eyes flashed with mischief as he said, "Hi, Monica. Don't you think you ought to get some clothes on?"

"I have clothes on," she said primly and patted her pajamas. "This is what I wear whenever we have a fire." Abruptly, she spun around and raced to her room. She had seen a taxi pulling up behind Laurita's Volkswagen. She grabbed a robe and slippers and returned in time to see her dad stepping out of the cab.

"Excuse me," she said breathlessly to Rob and El Pintor as she shot between them and down the steps toward her father. "Dad, you're here!" she cried and threw her arms around him. In a moment she moved away, rubbing her cheek. "Ugh. You haven't shaved."

"There wasn't time," he said somberly. Then, with a grin, "How about you, Miss Tanglehair? What happened to your ablutions this morning?"

"I just got up. They . . . they . . . oh, come on, Dad, Rob and Mr. Mead want to talk to you about the doors. And I have a lot to talk to you about, too."

"Absolutely. But not until I've had some coffee. Br-r-r-r. That stuff on the airplane."

Laurita and the two men were standing like a welcoming committee at the top of the steps. Laurita held out her hand and said, "I'm glad you're back, Eduardo. We have gallons of coffee. I had invited El . . . Señor Mead and

Roberto to breakfast with us. A measure of self-defense since the neighbors have showered us with food."

"They did?" Monica said in surprise. "When did all this happen?"

"It's almost eleven," Rob said with a grin that disappeared completely as he turned to Eduardo Ramos. "We haven't met, sir. I'm Roberto Almayo. My parents knew your wife well." He cleared his throat and threw Monica a quick look. "I know you have a lot to talk about, family stuff, so I think I'd better skip breakfast."

"Oh, no, you don't!" Laurita shot at him. "Not with all the food that's waiting."

"Well, there you have it," Eduardo Ramos said with a glimmer of a smile. "It seems you're our main hope in this food business. So I must insist you join us. Can the 'family stuff' wait, Monica?"

Monica shook her head briskly. "No, it can't wait. But maybe breakfast can. Why don't you just grab a cup of coffee while we talk?"

Three pairs of troubled eyes turned to Monica. Rob's gaze had quickly moved elsewhere, following his hand as it ran up and down the door frame. Her father's eyes showed surprise as did Laurita's.

As El Pintor looked at her, the blue of his eyes seemed to fade and turn gray, like the sky giving in to a storm. He took in a deep breath and expelled it. "Perhaps breakfast first is in order," he said quietly. "Your talk with your father might take some time, might require some . . . some explanation."

Monica gave him a quick glance. His brows were knitted in a worried frown. Impulsively, she reached for and squeezed his arm. "I doubt it," she said. "My father's the most forgiving man in the world." Then, because she had caught the questioning look on her dad's face, she added, "But he'll never forgive me if I'm rude again. Come on, let's all go in and eat."

"I should have known," Eduardo Ramos said to his daughter as he finished rereading El Pintor's letter. "All those long hours he spent at Cristina's bedside. If I hadn't been so torn up myself, I might have guessed."

Monica, seated on the floor of her bedroom, her knees pulled up to her chin, shook her head vigorously as she looked up at her dad who was sitting on the edge of her bed. "How could you have known? Only Laurita's father knew, and he didn't tell anyone, not until my mother and her parents had died."

It was more than an hour since they had finished breakfast. The five of them had eaten heartily and made only a small dent in the neighbors' offerings, offerings that included sweet egg bread from Lupe's *Panadería,* a bowl of homemade *chorizo* from the chunky lady across the street, and a wonderful casserole of eggs, cheese, and *chiles verdes* from the Almayos.

The discussion of the fire hadn't waited until after breakfast. In response to Eduardo Ramos's questions, and in between bites, they talked of Josie and how the confrontations with her had occurred. El Pintor said sadly that over the years he had learned that you win some and lose some, and that months back, he had given up on Josie. But he never dreamed that she would be capable of such a vicious act as arson. Or that her grudge against Monica was deep enough to drive her to it.

"She had it in for me, all right, Dad," Monica said. "After all, I'd caught her with the paints that night and had to use the hose to stop her. Then we'd gotten her pal Licha interested in planting flowers instead of hanging with her. And to crown it all, I'd made her cry 'uncle'—don't ask me how I did it; it was pure luck—when she was set on beating me up. But let's forget Josie. Do you suppose there's a cinnamon roll left?"

When they were through eating, Laurita insisted that she would take care of the cleanup, that El Pintor and Rob still had the back door and back steps to check out, and Monica had to bring her father up to date on all that had been happening. No one could move her away from that decision, and that's how it had been settled.

Now, Monica, from her vantage point on the bedroom floor, studied her father's face and said, "Dad? Does it make you angry? What he did, I mean. Giving up his baby like that."

"Angry? No, honey. His letter explained his state of mind clearly, a state of mind I can understand. Maybe I didn't have such deep feelings of guilt when your mother

died as he did when he lost his wife, but I can sense what he was going through. I was a little crazy myself the first few months after your mother's death. Perhaps he made a big mistake in giving up Cristina. Perhaps. But maybe not. She was a lucky girl to have been surrounded by three loving adults as she was growing up. I worry about leaving you so much. And I guess I've been right to have that worry. Look at the problems you've had to face alone in the last few weeks. I feel as if I'd deserted you."

"Oh, no, Dad!" Monica jumped up to sit on the bed beside him. "On the contrary. You gave me a special opportunity." She grinned as she added, "It's like those wilderness tests some kids are given. You know, where they're dumped and have to live on their own in the wilderness for a while. I don't mean that Lucia Street is a wilderness—although it *is* different—or that I was really alone, but I had to make some decisions and take some actions all by myself, and that's been good for me. And, Dad," she added, leaning her head on his shoulder, "I always knew that you were there."

He put his arm around her and gave her a squeeze. In a moment he stood up. "Let's go welcome your grandfather into the family," he said.

They went around the side of the house to find El Pintor and Rob pounding on the back steps' railing. The midday sun glistened off of El Pintor's white hair as he straightened up and turned toward them. Her father, his hand outstretched, strode to him. Monica had trouble keeping tears back as he gave El Pintor a huge hug and said, "I'm glad to greet you, sir. In your new role, that is. I'm very glad that you're a part of our family."

When El Pintor pulled a rumpled white handkerchief from his back pocket, removed his glasses, and dabbed at his eyes, her father quickly said, "Tell me about these steps. Will they all have to be replaced?"

Rob, who was standing beside Monica, took her hand and pressed it tightly, and they both grinned at Laurita, who was looking down at them through the screen door.

Later that afternoon Monica, her father, and El Pintor walked up to Chimney Hill.

"I always wanted to leave this property to Cristina," El Pintor said to Eduardo Ramos as they started off, "and if I had, it would now belong to you. So, when I say that I am deeding it to Monica, I don't want you to object."

"To me?" Monica said. "I'm the one who'll object. You could sell it. And get a bundle of money, I'll bet."

"And what would I do with that bundle?"

"Why . . . why, travel, of course."

"I did all my traveling when I was young, my dear. My traveling days have long been over. All I want now, if you'll both allow it, is to remain where I am, to paint and watch my young friends grow."

"Monica is right, Mr. Mead," her father said. "That property could be very valuable."

"I hope it is," El Pintor said. "And I won't feel like a member of the family until you allow Monica to accept it and start calling me Frank."

"All right, all right, Frank," her father said, "that's easily done. But as to the property, we'll have to discuss that later."

Monica heard what her father and El Pintor were saying, but she was more interested in what César and his sister Licha might be discussing in their front yard across the street. Licha, it seemed, was trying to persuade César of something, but César, his feet firmly planted, was shaking his head vigorously. Licha shrugged and turned abruptly. She gave the tire that hung from their big tree a push and set it to swinging. Then, with a toss of her head, she walked leisurely across the street.

"Hi, Monica," she said as she reached them. "I heard about the fire and about Josie. And I want you to know that I didn't have anything to do with it. Honest. I wanted César to tell you that I was home all night 'cause I figured you'd believe him. Anyway, I was. My cousins are here from Mexico, and we were up practically the whole night talking and laughing. We even heard the fire engines, but we thought they were on another street."

Monica looked helplessly at El Pintor, and he said, "We believe you, Licha. That fire was Josie's doing. You wouldn't do anything like that."

"Dad," Monica said, "this is Licha Gámez. She . . . she helped us plant some flowers along the side of the house."

"I'm glad to know you, young lady," Eduardo Ramos said. "That was kind of you."

Licha nodded in his direction, then said, "Did the fire ruin the flowers we planted?"

"I don't know," Monica answered. "I haven't looked."

El Pintor said, "They're fine, they're fine. I think they're taking hold. Which reminds me. I'll be getting my paintings ready for a show in the next few weeks, and I'll need someone to weed and water my flower beds. I was wondering if . . . well, are you by any chance available to give me a hand with that?"

"Me?" Licha said, and her olive-brown face turned a rosy pink. "Well, . . . I guess . . . sure, I can do that."

"I'll pay you something, of course," El Pintor said. "We'll talk more later. Come down and see me."

It seemed to Monica that an amazing change had taken place in Licha. Suddenly, she was prettier. But not just prettier, she was softer somehow. "Sure. Okay. I'll be there," Licha said, and, with no goodbyes, turned and tore across the street.

Up on Chimney Hill the sea breeze was more brisk and had a touch of coolness that was welcome. They walked around the disintegrating cement foundation to the summerhouse.

"This is quite a place, Frank," Eduardo Ramos said as he stood admiring the view. "No wonder you hung on to it."

"I thought of selling it once or twice. I wanted to give Ramón and Chita some of the proceeds, but they would have none of it. So I told them I would leave the property to Cristina with or without their consent. That they'd have to grin and bear it. Come along, come along, Eduardo, I want to show you the other side of the hill."

Monica smiled. "I'll wait for you here," she said and watched her father and her grandfather go down the summerhouse steps and disappear around the shrubbery.

Looking out at the little bits of sparkling ocean that she could see and listening to the diminishing voices of the two men, Monica felt at peace. Or, at least, at ease. In any case, it was a sense of well-being such as she had not experienced in a long, long time. It had to do, she was sure, with all that had happened since she had come to Lucia. The couple of weeks she had spent here seemed a much longer time than that, and El Pintor, Laurita, Rob, Toni, César, and even the chunky woman across the street seemed like people she had known in a time that was not measured in hours or days or weeks, but in the depth of the experiences that they had shared. She was sure that if tomorrow she was to leave Lucia and never see any of them again, they would always be an important part of her.

But she wasn't leaving tomorrow. Nor the next day. Nor the next. And she was glad. Because there was so much to look forward to. For one, her dad was going to be home a lot this summer. So was Rob. Besides, she told herself with a smile, there'd be new doors and a new paint job on the house. Then, a party for El Pintor to celebrate his new family and the exhibition of his paintings, a party for which Laurita and Toni were already making up a long guest list. And how about the flowers they'd planted along the side of the house, the ones she'd thought would never grow? Were those little sticks of geraniums really "taking hold" like El Pintor had told Licha they were? Well, why not? It seemed that Monica was "taking hold," too. And the summer was just beginning.